TRINITY

THE
ASSASSIN

ZACK SATRIANI

*Hodder
Children's
Books*

A division of Hachette Children's Books

Copyright © 2012 Hothouse Fiction Ltd

Produced by Hothouse Fiction – www.hothousefiction.com

First published in Great Britain in 2012
by Hodder Children's Books

The author's moral rights are hereby asserted.

1

A Catalogue record for this book is available from the British Library

ISBN 978 1 444 90661 5

Typeset in AGaramond Book by Avon DataSet Ltd,
Bidford on Avon, Warwickshire

Printed and bound in Great Britain by
CPI Group (UK) Ltd, Croydon, CR0 4YY

The paper and board used in this paperback by Hodder Children's Books
are natural recyclable products made from wood grown in
sustainable forests. The manufacturing processes conform to the
environmental regulations of the country of origin.

Hodder Children's Books
a division of Hachette Children's Books
338 Euston Road, London NW1 3BH
An Hachette UK company
www.hachette.co.uk

With special thanks to Adrian Bott

Prologue

Leagues away from the interplanetary trade lanes, the immense dead moon drifted through space like a wreck crossing fathomless seas. Life had made a start upon its craggy surface once, before abandoning the fight to survive.

Though long dead, the moon was never silent. The thin atmosphere gathered itself into winds which howled around the sharp rocks, swirling grey dust into ghostly forms.

But the army of horrors that now clustered in a crater on the moon's dark side were no ghosts. Rank upon rank went marching up and down: spider-bodied creatures with whip-like arms and pincers that could crush even the strongest plasteel. They clambered easily across the rocky landscape on long, spindly legs, as ugly as locusts but as efficient as assassins.

Above the crater crouched a humanoid figure in black armour. He nodded in satisfaction as the spider-like aliens went marching past below. As soon as they reached him they stopped, standing in perfect formation.

Such impressive weapons, he thought. *Tough, adaptable, lethal. But no weapon is more important than the hand that wields it.*

'Execute Formation 937,' he said, thinking the words at them as he spoke.

The ranks of aliens chittered and moved into a new arrangement. Those in front spaced themselves out, while the rearmost ranks held back, ready to spring.

The watching figure pressed a control on his wrist. From the other side of the crater a huge robot rose up from beneath the dust. It was shaped like a crab's shell on two squat legs, with barrels of devastating weapons poking out from beneath its carapace.

Click, click, whirrrr went the cannons as they warmed up. The robot fired, sending the aliens scattering. The front ranks instantly began to scuttle here and there in a seemingly random dash. The rear ranks waited, tense, biding their time.

More cannon fire blasted the front rank, but their wide spacing meant even a successful hit only destroyed one or two at a time. The robot's heavy guns were almost useless against an enemy too light and fast to track.

Without warning, the rear ranks charged. They rushed at the robot in a tide of segmented limbs and gnashing mandibles. They attacked its legs with jabs and hacks, causing oil and sparks to jet out.

The robot snatched up the leaping aliens and crushed them in its grippers before dropping their mangled bodies to the ground. But they were upon it now, tearing at its motivator cables, biting at its piston shafts.

In a single surge, they pulled the battle machine over on to its back. Scuttling back into formation, the troops ripped out cables and components like trophies.

A gutted shell now lay where the robot had fallen.

The watching figure smacked a fist into his palm. *Already they begin to master the tactics of formation combat*, he thought. *They are learning faster than anyone could have guessed. It is time for some more field experience.*

'Board the ships,' he commanded. 'Prepare to go to war. Orgren is our next target.'

1

Keller banked his sleek fighter round the curving canyon wall. He held the joystick one-handed with the steady, assured grip of a champion racer, even though the speed of the turn made it judder. A novice would have clutched it tight with both white-knuckled hands.

'Let's see them follow me in here,' he muttered.

He wound around an S-shaped bend, breathing evenly despite the walls of rock hurling themselves in his path. Just as he thought he'd escaped them, three sinister blips appeared on the rear-view screen behind him.

'Krack,' he swore. 'Don't you scum-suckers ever give up?'

The three other fighters were threading through the canyon, trying to lock on to him. They were elite Aurax strike craft, shaped like scythe-winged darts, armed with double plasma guns.

And they wanted him dead.

Plasma rounds peppered the air around him. Keller swung his ship from side to side, evading the blasts easily.

Keller grinned. 'Catch me if you can . . . ship, give me *full* thrust!'

He was flung back in his seat and the canyon became a blur. Keller went into the next bend screaming with glee, his ship's wings carving the air like a double blade.

Warning lights flashed, begging him to eject.

He ignored them.

The Aurax fighters put on a fresh burst of speed too, struggling to catch up. They fired. Again, Keller rolled out of the way. Their sprays of plasma fire scorched black marks down the canyon walls.

One of them took the bend too fast, struck a rocky outcrop and exploded in a dramatic crimson-orange fireball.

Keller whooped. 'One down!'

An ominous *beep beep beep* cut his rapture short. Flashing red text across his heads-up display read INCOMING MISSILE.

'Oh no,' he stammered. 'Not a mini-nuke. Not now!'

The joystick was suddenly slippery in his hand. Once a mini-nuke locked on, you were finished.

Keller banked his ship sideways to shoot through a sudden narrow section of canyon. The missile followed a fraction of a click later, followed by the lead Aurax fighter.

The one in the rear failed to turn in time. Its wings were torn off by the narrow walls, and the remains flew like a flaming javelin to explode far below.

One enemy left. But the missile would hit his ship in three clicks.

There was only one thing for it, and it would take impeccable timing. As a warning beep screeched, Keller pulled back on the joystick and dived towards the canyon floor. At the very last moment, he jerked his craft up again.

The missile hit the rocky ground, exploding in a thunderous blast and missing him by a whisker. Keller was safe, but still the frantic *beep beep beeping* continued. Was there another enemy craft?

As the noise became more urgent, Keller realized it was coming from his wrist. Glancing down at his beeping wrist-com, Keller rolled his eyes. Great. He was wanted in the royal audience chamber. Duty called.

The screens around him went blank. 'Simulation terminated,' said the soft digital voice of his Holo-Entertainment GamesTerminal Plus, or as his father had always called it, 'That blasted box you practically live in.'

Ten minutes later, he stood facing a thin man who was pointing a laser device at him.

'Your Majesty, I'm going to have to ask you to put your hands up.'

The thin man pointing the device at Keller sounded genuinely apologetic. Keller rolled his eyes and lazily took a bite of the cake he held in one hand. It was dripping with pink chrestiberry icing, just the thing for a royal breakfast.

Chewing thoughtfully, he held his arms up as the royal tailor adjusted the holo-scanner. Needle-thin beams shot from the device and traced Keller's body shape in a luminous grid, scanning every contour, feeding his measurements back to the handheld unit.

Keller glanced over at the heap of rich crimson fabric that was halfway to becoming his coronation gown, and grinned to himself. It was Tevekarian brocade, so costly that a seat covering made from it could cost more than a whole ship, and yet he'd bought it for a tenth of the asking price.

The holo-scanner gave a beep, jolting Keller out of his reverie. 'What's wrong?' he demanded.

'Oh, nothing, nothing,' the tailor said breezily. 'Just

a little discrepancy. As I expected, your old measurements are no longer valid. I had no new data to work with, you see.' He sighed. 'So much has changed in the last moon. Your father's tragic death, the upheavals in galactic trade . . .'

'Can you get to the point? I'm supposed to be meeting with two senior traders right about now!'

The tailor glanced at the cake in Keller's hand. 'I'll have to let the waistband out a bit,' he said in a pained tone.

Keller sighed, took one last bite and reluctantly dropped the cake on to a plate. He pushed his jet-black hair out of his face and frowned at his reflection. His strong jaw and sharp nose were so much like his father's. But while King Lial had always exuded an aura of confidence, Keller just saw a worried teenager staring back at him.

As the tailor fitted the cloth around him, holding it in place with grav-pins, Keller gazed out of the huge window that took up the whole west wall. It was bright morning and the streets of the city below were bustling with life. The sky overhead was empty, an endless peaceful blue.

A moment later, the peace was broken as the sleek silver lance-shape of a racing ship screamed past, leaving a wide white exhaust trail in its wake. Keller sighed. His own racing ship, a top-of-the-line Mazakomi, was gathering dust in its hangar – well, not literally gathering dust, because the frictionless forcefield wouldn't let any settle. He couldn't imagine when he'd get to fly it again. He felt a deep, painful longing to be out there, tearing up the skies in the Mazakomi racer, far away from the world of duty.

But duty, unlike gravity, was impossible to escape. He tore himself away from his daydreams. The tailor had finished; now there was work to do.

'Send them in,' he said into the intercom.

Two men came storming into the room, shouting at one another. One was Tyrus, the bristly old head of the Trade Council; the other was Yall, who everybody knew had his eye on the same position.

'The coronation is a crucial opportunity to rebuild good relations with Quisnov 4!' Yall insisted, jabbing a finger at a printout of a seating plan.

'You're suggesting we insult the Cibarians? Are they to sit at the edge and beg for scraps?' Tyrus roared.

Yall appealed directly to Keller. 'Your Majesty, with all respect to Tyrus, his plan will be a diplomatic disaster!'

As the yelling began afresh, Keller felt his heart sink.

His father would have known what to do. He wished he could ask the old trade king's advice, but he could never do that again. Well, he'd just have to fall back on his own skills.

'Gentlemen!' said Keller, surprising himself with the authority in his voice. Both men stopped arguing on the spot, and looked at him. 'I suggest a compromise. Let the Cibarians have the foremost seats at the coronation, to show them how welcome they are. Then afterwards, at the feast, the delegates from Quisnov 4 can join us at the high table and reaffirm our bonds of friendship. That's honour enough for everyone, don't you think?'

Tyrus scratched his beard and thought for a long time. 'Not a bad solution, I'll give you that,' he declared.

Yall shrugged. 'I have no objection. The feast is, after all, the more important event.'

As Tyrus began to argue the point, Keller twisted his father's ring around his finger, wishing it could somehow summon him back. There was still a dark, aching vacuum in his heart where Trade King Lial ought to be. His sudden, violent death caused by the Nara-Karith was hard enough to accept, without having to step into his shoes too. Keller had barely had time to mourn his father. Now he was expected to take his place.

He clenched his fist around the ring. Grieving would have to wait. Without strong leadership, Cantor would tear itself into a million squabbling pieces.

Iccus, the commander-in-chief of the Bellori, swung his great armoured head from left to right, surveying his assembled generals. They stood gathered in the glow of a central star chart surrounded by holo-globes that bathed the room in volcanic red light. The chart showed the planet Bellus, orbited by transparent hosts of silvery darts – the Bellori fleet. There were no seats. Sitting was for those too old, crippled or weak to fight.

Iccus's teenage daughter, Dray, stood among the others. Like them, she wore grey armour made up of overlapping, ridged keratin plates – resistant to nearly any blade and most energy weapons. A Bellori helmet hid her fair hair and eyes that flashed with passion and intelligence. She knew the meaning of every symbol on the astro-chart, from the frigates to the fighters.

'Sudor has betrayed and dishonoured us,' General Iccus began, getting straight to the point. 'When the Nara-Karith captured the leaders of the three Trinity planets, he would not attack to save us. He put his own thirst for power before the security of Bellus. Let the void have his bones.'

12

Fists thumped chests in the traditional sign of approval. Armour plates rattled.

'He remains a threat. Sudor possesses information about our ongoing defence of Bellus, and of the entire Trinity System. We must therefore change our strategy.' With a swoop of his hand, Iccus detached a cluster of icons from the main group. 'The ships he commanded must be reassigned.'

He struck the pommel of his sword once with his fist, to show he had finished and discussion could begin.

Dray clenched her jaw as the generals began offering predictable, unimaginative suggestions for the best defence of the system, doling out Sudor's ships to other commanders.

One after another, the plans followed. Old Brancur even tried to roll out his ridiculous 'Wall of Iron' idea yet again, which would have seen Bellus surrounded by a triple ring of dreadnoughts while Cantor and Aquanthis were assigned a handful of near obsolete fighters. To Dray's relief, Brancur was not allowed to speak for long.

In that moment of silence, she saw her chance and took it. 'We can't divide up Sudor's fleet like a pack of Cantorian merchants sharing out grain!' she insisted. 'Those crews know each other. They have fought

13

together, shed blood together. They fight as one. It would be dishonourable and inefficient to redistribute them.' She took a breath then spoke again quickly before anyone could interrupt. 'I propose we designate Sudor's ships as a new deep patrol fleet, to act as the first line of defence against hostiles from outside the system. They can use Therek Station as a supply post.'

Silence followed for a few clicks, then General Vrax spoke. 'Nobody questions Brancur's valour in battle,' he said, 'but the Wall of Iron is simply not viable . . .'

It was as if she hadn't said anything at all. Dray bit down so hard her teeth began to ache.

The discussion wore on. Eventually General Scraa addressed the council. 'It is always better to keep a fleet intact than to dismantle it. I say we assign Sudor's ships to patrol the whole Trinity System. Therek Station can keep them supplied and fuelled.'

Immediately the assembled Bellori began to thump their chests in approval. Inside her armoured helmet, Dray bared her teeth. It was her idea, just said in a slightly different way. How *dare* they.

'Excellent,' said Iccus. 'Invasion from outside the system must be our prime—'

Dray hurled a foot-long *scratha* knife.

It pierced the map dead centre, shattering the glass

14

screen. Stars and ships vanished. Sparks skittered like comets across the table's suddenly dark surface.

Breathing heavily, Dray looked from warrior to silent warrior. Finally, she had their attention.

'I demand to be recognized,' she said thickly. 'Father, I defended Bellus from the Nara-Karith! I killed the queen with my own blade! You should reward me by giving me the military position I deserve!' She glanced around. 'Does anyone here dare to say different?'

'You fought bravely,' Iccus said. 'Nobody denies that. But you will not see active military duty. You are too important.'

Too important? Dray couldn't believe what she was hearing.

'We cannot risk you,' croaked old Brancur. 'You are your father's heir.'

General Vrax nodded. 'It is best that you remain away from combat, for the sake of Bellus.'

Dray slammed her fist on the ruined table and felt the glass crack.

'*Away?* Through combat, I won my rightful place on this Admiralty Council!' she raged. 'Have you all forgotten who defeated Sudor in the blood challenge? I did! I proved I was stronger than your second-in-command, Father – his place rightfully belongs to *me*!'

Dray would not listen to any more empty words. She stormed out of the room. As she went, she smashed her fists together as hard as she could, and the crash of armour on armour echoed around the council chamber in her wake.

Deep below the rolling surface of Aquanthis, Ayl slept uneasily. His slender, blue-skinned body twitched, like an eel caught in a net. He thrashed in the bed of long shara-weeds where he lay, and moaned.

As if trapped in an endless time loop, his mind returned to the same moment: Dray, sprawled on the floor. The alien rearing up over her. The k-gun, cold in his hands. Pulling the trigger.

And then the death.

In his mind, he saw the spray of yellow, the explosion of fragments. It had been a living creature. And he had killed it.

Ayl cried out in his sleep, and blinked himself awake. A familiar presence washed over him then, soothing, calming. Just as she had done when he was a newtling, she slowed his pulse rate and smoothed away the nightmarish images reeling in his brain. Ayl's breathing gradually calmed, his gills opening and shutting less frantically.

You shouldn't need mother's intervention at your age, Ayl. Lady Moa's thoughts were warm but a little impatient, like diving from warm upper waters into colder ones.

I didn't ask for it, Ayl thought back testily. Free from his nightmares, he felt a little foolish now.

Practise your meditative disciplines, she suggested. *Perform Joh-II-Noor, the ordering of the self.*

You think I haven't? Ayl responded. *I meditate every morning. It's not enough. I took a life, mother. The only life that thing ever had.*

His mother became stern. *Leave the past in the past, my son. There is no danger here, no bloodshed. You are on Aquanthis, and you are safe.*

The light of a new day was filtering down through the waves. Even among its beauty Ayl felt haunted, ill at ease. Soon it would be time to join the others in morning prayer. In the great meeting of Aquanth minds his pain would vanish; it would wash away, as all individual things did.

The undersea temple, a huge coral pyramid encrusted with crystalline growths, was not far away. Ayl swam towards it, comforted by the familiar sights of his home. A shoal of kallin were passing by, their butterfly fins refracting the light, their long electric tails trailing like neon streamers into the dark. As Ayl swam over a crevasse, the call of a tame kyassid came echoing up from beneath, and he saw the creature's beak gape up at him. A tentacle zoomed playfully towards him and he dodged it with a silvery laugh.

The temple was already filling up. Ayl called a greeting to the group of Aquanths in the antechamber, but nobody returned it. They would not look him in the eye. The feeling of dread began to steal back over him.

Ayl sat cross-legged on the marble seat, waiting for the naptarch, the high priestess's closest advisor, to begin morning prayers. More and more Aquanths entered and took their seats, but none sat near him. Gloomy and alone, like a rock surrounded by sea, he could only sit and wait.

Across the temple, Ayl saw a familiar figure. Wan! There was Wan, his best friend, at last! Wan looked up and caught Ayl's eye, and in that instant their minds made contact.

Hey, podbrother! Ayl thought. *What's wrong with everyone today?*

I'm sorry, Ayl, Wan thought back, full of misery. *I shouldn't be talking to you.*

Says who?

18

Wan's thoughts seeped guiltily out of him. *My parents, the priesthood, everyone! They say you're dangerous.*

Ayl was horrified. *Dangerous? How long have you known me, Wan? We studied together. We hatched together!*

Don't make me feel even worse about this! Wan begged. *They say you are damaging the consciousness . . .*

How am I damaging it? Ayl was half despairing and half furious.

I'm going to have to show you, Wan thought. *Look, Ayl. This is how you seem to us.*

In a flash, Ayl saw what Wan saw – what all the others could see.

They could all sense the moment he'd killed the alien, and it revolted them. To Aquanths, his mind was like a festering wound. Violence writhed in it like rotworms in a whale carcass. The same act of murder that horrified him so was turning him into an outcast.

Ayl, I'm so sorry. I can't let you join with me, Wan said. *But I will pray for you.*

As the ancient, wrinkled naptarch began the service, the Aquanths chanted their song of praise to the morning, their minds linked in harmony. They sang of the unity of life. All things were holy; all things had a rightful place.

But nobody wanted to join minds with Ayl. Nobody

wanted to be tainted by his vile, ugly memories, full of blood and horror. As their minds joyously embraced, leaving him unwanted and rejected, Ayl realized he had never felt so alone.

2

'Your Majesty!' called a lurking attendant, just as Keller came striding around the corner. 'The Director of Protocol needs to see you urgently.'

'Well, I don't want to see him.'

'I must insist!'

Keller cursed to himself. 'I spent all of yesterday with the man! He told me he'd seen to everything. What more can he want?'

The attendant was forced to keep pace with him, huffing and puffing in the heat. 'The Royal Mint urgently needs your approval for an official image.'

'Image?' Keller snapped, not pausing in his stride.

'An image of you, Your Majesty! For the coin of the realm! As the newly crowned trade king, your face must replace your father's on all of our coins.'

Keller suddenly felt even more irritable than he already had. 'I'm sure they've done a lovely job of my face. Consider it approved.'

'You, ah, have to actually *see* it to approve it . . .'

'Why do we even bother with coins any more?' demanded Keller. 'Everyone uses digital data slates.'

'Tradition, of course! The quantanium coins of Cantor represent our prosperity, reaching back through many glorious generations of successful business! Remember, you will not just be a king, but a trade king!'

'Well, isn't that a coincidence. I'm on my way to the director of protocol right now,' Keller lied, putting on a fresh burst of speed. 'Off you go.'

'But his office is in the other direction . . .'

Keller kept walking briskly until the man's voice faded away.

The palace guards saluted as he passed. He stared straight ahead, trying to look as if he had somewhere very important to be. Guards usually left you alone if you did that, and didn't ask troublesome questions.

The archway ahead led into the private palace grounds, several square kilopaces of preserved countryside behind a domed forcefield. Keller could taste the fresh air already and hurried towards it.

The palace felt as if it were crushing him under its stifling weight. Tradition, bureaucracy and responsibility burying him like a shipload of plasteel girders. He couldn't hold it all up. Desperate for freedom, he broke into a run.

Suddenly, as if he'd fled through a rift into another world, he was running across open lawns under a clear sky. Sprinklers gushed rainbows into the air, and marble statues gazed at him serenely from their pedestals. Rows of exotic flowers, brought from distant star systems at great expense, nodded brightly under the strong sun. The waters of an ornamental pool flashed briefly with gemstone colours: captive kallin fish from Aquanthis.

Keller scrambled to the top of a green hillock and stood looking out at his lands, breathing freely at last. The family's private hunting woods lay ahead, dark and promising. He knew his oldest friend, Zaff, would be there at the lodge, waiting patiently for him.

That's right. Bolt for the forests like a hunted animal, he thought. *Back to the dark tangled places you know better than anyone.*

He looked back over his shoulder at the palace, and felt a pang of guilt. He belonged in there, even if it meant being pestered and measured and badgered from one end of the day to the other. All this luxury and open air, all the special privileges he'd always taken for granted . . . they all went hand in hand with his fate. He was born to be dressed up, put on display and forced to do whatever the Trade Council demanded. He'd always known this was the future that awaited him, but didn't think he'd have to deal with it while he was still a teenager.

He ought to go back. It was what his father would have expected of him.

Instead, he ran down to the welcome shade of the woods. A little way inside, he found the royal hunting lodge, with a familiar shape chained up outside. The sleek red creature raised its head as Keller approached, watching him with eyes of silver. Its sharp diamond teeth glinted, but its tail lashed the leaves happily.

'Hey, Zaff. Good boy!' Keller loosed the chain and the Inui hunting hound ran up alongside him, snuffling his hand in greeting. If he hadn't been the hound's master, his hand would be lying in the leaves right now.

Keller found a stick to throw and flung it as far as he could. Instantly Zaff ran to fetch it, streaking away like a tracker missile. Keller watched him grab the stick and run back with it, then drop it at his feet. Big silver eyes begged for his approval.

Keller smiled and scratched Zaff's ears. 'Well done. Good boy.'

This is my real kingdom, Keller thought. *And Zaff's one subject I know I can trust.*

* * *

'Orbital clearance granted, General Iccus. On behalf of the Cantorian Spacefarers' Guild, may I be the first to welcome you to our planet on this joyous—'

The Bellori leader silenced the com. 'Making planetfall in sixty clicks,' he said without looking behind him. He eased back on a throttle and the turbulence of Cantor's atmosphere began to thrum against the ship's underside.

Eight of the other members of the Bellori delegation buckled their webbing harnesses. Normally Dray would have joined them; there was no honour in taking unnecessary risks, after all. But not today.

Dray sat sullen and silent at the very back of the ship, crammed between two cargo racks in preference to a seat. The space was cramped and smelled of engine oil. She did not care. Her *scratha* knife had reached razor sharpness ten minutes ago, but she kept sharpening it, watching the sparks fly. It passed the time.

The weapons clipped to the wall were starting to rattle, but she paid them no attention. Her father liked rough landings. They added some excitement to the dullness of routine space flight, which was mostly automated. It seemed this one was going to be especially rough, as if he were making a point. To her.

Well, let him jostle them all around if he chose. She had already decided not to give him the satisfaction of resuming her seat.

The com-link gave a shrill beep. Iccus thumped it immediately. 'Speak.'

The helmeted head of a Bellori commander appeared on the screen, with a bank of monitors behind him. 'Apologies, General, but we have an update on the Zarix situation. We've just heard from the Sandashti communications hub. Another of our patrols is no longer responding to coms.'

Zarix. Dray searched her memory for the name and found it. It was a dead moon, stellar leagues away from the three planets of the Trinity System, used for observation.

'Time and content of the last com received?'

'Four cycles ago. Confirmation of order to investigate the last two Zarix patrols that failed to report in.'

Iccus was silent for a while. 'Have you investigated possible sources of coms disruption?'

'Our records show no space phenomena in the region capable of blocking a com signal. I believe we can rule out hardware failure. Hostile action is the most logical explanation. I've forwarded the earlier reports.'

'It may be a feint, to lure us away and leave Cantor vulnerable.'

Dray shook her head. That didn't sound right to her. If someone wanted to draw Bellori forces away from Cantor, they would have been openly hostile. Not this silence. It wasn't provocative enough.

The officer on the screen turned to answer a question from an unseen colleague, then turned back to Iccus. 'Sir, we have volunteers willing to lead an expeditionary force.'

'Noted. No military action to be taken at this time, Commander. Our presence is required here at the coronation. For now, carry out a thorough equipment test. I want to eliminate even the smallest possibility of mechanical failure.'

'Understood, sir.'

'Keep me updated. Out.' Iccus steered the ship further into Cantor's atmosphere. A whining noise began as the cooling systems fought to keep the hull from burning up.

Dray knew she didn't know the whole story, and it angered her. 'Father?' she shouted above the noise. 'What's happening on Zarix? What did the other reports say?'

'What may or may not be happening there is not

your concern,' he said. 'You have a role. I suggest you play it.'

The ship lurched. Dray grabbed a hanging strap, lightning-fast, and managed to stay on her feet.

'We have not discussed a *role*,' she said through gritted teeth.

'This is a diplomatic event, and you will show the proper respect by acting diplomatically,' said Iccus. 'You are the child of a planetary leader. Sit near the trade king. Catch up on old times. Do whatever you have to do to establish goodwill with the new order.'

' "Whatever I have to do?" ' said Dray, sensing his meaning and feeling a surge of cold anger. Did he think she was a royal prize, a token to be given away?

Iccus gave a harsh laugh. 'You will have to be more approachable than that, girl. Bellus, Cantor and Aquanthis are allies, don't forget. We protect them, in return for water from Aquanthis and goods from Cantor. We must all do our duty and make the Trinity System alliance stronger than ever before, for this generation – and for future ones.'

The Cantorian woman's smile was beginning to crack. She was still holding out her hands. 'I assure you, Your Holiness, we intend no offence, but *all* items have to be scanned, it's basic spaceport security procedure.'

Ayl's mother, Lady Moa, the High Priestess of Aquanthis, gripped the pearl sceptre she was carrying even more tightly. The group of Aquanth delegates surrounding her looked on, their faces patient and inscrutable.

'I am sorry, child,' she said. 'This is a sacred object. It must pass from my hands *directly* into the new trade king's, to symbolize our recognition of his leadership.'

'I'll only need to take it for a moment! If you'll just come this way . . .'

Through their telepathic connection, Ayl could actually feel his mother's mighty calm radiating from her. It was like swimming alongside one of the ocean's elder leviathans, all wisdom and serenity.

'If I placed this sceptre in *your* hands, young lady, it would mean that all of Aquanthis recognized *you* as the new ruler of Cantor.' A twinkle of amusement flashed in Lady Moa's eyes. 'That would be . . . unfortunate, do you not think?'

Another Cantorian attendant came to the woman's rescue. 'There's a remote scanner in the main office. Run and fetch it, quickly!' He gave Ayl's mother an obsequious grin. 'I'm so sorry to keep you, Your Holiness, it really is just standard procedure. I'm sure you don't have a laser rifle or anything hidden in that sceptre, ha ha.'

'Indeed,' said the Aquanth high priestess, giving the attendant an appraising look. Ayl heard her thought to the other Aquanths: *The sacred sceptre conceal a weapon? I weep for these people.*

Ayl watched the Cantorians bustling around the immense, noisy spaceport. Something was obviously very wrong here. Everyone seemed to be trying to do too much at once, while finding someone else to blame for it.

Can such a bumbling species really be the equal of the Aquanths? thought one of the delegates. *They are just so unevolved. They go about communicating with words all the time, little better than animal grunts.*

Another delegate chimed in: *And they don't even have the beginnings of telepathic ability! Imagine spending your whole life with no mind but your own to talk to, locked in your own skull like a prisoner!*

Ayl knew that was wrong. *I spent time with a Bellorian and a Cantorian*, he protested. *They ARE capable of telepathy, though it is dormant in them.*

The other Aquanths in the delegation looked at him with distaste. *We would prefer it if you kept your thoughts to yourself, Ayl. We have no desire to share your memories.*

30

'Ah, we are blessed at last.' Ayl's mother sighed as the scanner was finally found and used. Minutes later, they were changing into their ceremonial robes in a private chamber. Their gauzy, shimmery clothing was meant to be worn underwater, where it would billow and move with the currents. On land, it just sagged.

Ayl felt much the same himself. Each breath of air hurt his lungs; it was like breathing smoke. He knew he'd get used to it, just like he had before, but he couldn't look at the ornamental ponds and pools of Cantor without craving a breath of water. And his webbed feet, which powered him through water so gracefully, felt clumsy on land.

'This way,' an attendant fussed, as they emerged from the changing room. 'We're, ah, almost ready to begin. There have been a few, ah, complications, but nothing anyone need worry about . . .'

He led them down a hallway carpeted in blue to the throne room, a vast hollow orb of marble and gold. Seats led down into it in descending tiers, all of them encrusted with gems and precious fitments, and the dignitaries of many worlds were already filing into them. They were like the coral formations of Aquanthis, except those were natural and free to everyone.

This whole place is like one huge boast, Ayl thought.

31

We are richest; we are the most prosperous; we are the best.

He saw the Aquanth banner hanging above a row of sculpted translucent blue thrones. That was where they would sit to watch Keller become King. Ayl looked around, but Keller himself was nowhere in sight. There was Dray, though, and the Bellori contingent. He raised a hand in greeting and, to his surprise, she gave a stiff salute in return.

Despite the insane displays of wealth and the fuss and red tape, Ayl felt relieved. It was better to be an alien here on Cantor, where everything was strange and different, than to feel like an alien among his own people.

His nightmares had been hanging over him like an inky shroud, and he was sick of it. Sick of the rejection, sick of the feelings of dread. It wasn't just the bloody violence in his past that haunted him, but the gnawing certainty that something even worse was around the corner, waiting to happen. It had made him a pariah.

He relaxed into his chair and practised his air breathing. *It's good to be away from Aquanthis*, he thought.

A flash of anxious concern cut across his mind. Not his. His mother's. She had overheard his thoughts.

You are Aquanth, she told him telepathically. *Don't*

celebrate being away from our home. Our strength is in our unity. We stand together.

Ayl sank back, chastened but still relieved. Nobody on Cantor was telepathic. At least here he could walk through the crowds without anyone sensing his memories and recoiling in disgust. For a people that supposedly stood together, the Aquanths were pretty keen to shove him away.

Keller slipped in through a rear door, just as a blast of trumpets announced the arrival of the last of the guests. He still had time to reach the throne room.

Ducking around a corner, he nearly ran smack into Tyrus. The man loomed over him, arms folded.

'Nice of you to put in an appearance at your own coronation, boy!' he roared. 'Where in the seven hells have you been? This whole place is in an uproar because of you!'

'Can't you organize anything without me standing over you?' Keller said with a smirk.

Tyrus's nostrils flared. 'This is nothing to joke about. Do you realize we thought you might have been abducted? After everything that's already happened, don't you realize the danger you're in?'

Keller thought back to how worried he was when his

father was abducted by the Nara-Karith. But he wasn't going to give Tyrus the satisfaction of an apology. He shrugged, 'I'm here now, aren't I? So let's get on with it.'

Tyrus shook his head in disbelief. 'At least your father isn't here to see you disgrace your coronation day,' he hissed. 'He'd be ashamed of you.'

'No, Tyrus, he is not here,' said Keller coldly. 'I am. And you will remember your place in future.'

He strode off ahead of Tyrus, his heart pounding. Shame was burning him up from within. There were no more arrogant words left to say. There was only the ceremony, and what it meant. He couldn't escape his duty now. He had to go through with it.

He went to his private room to change. Swallowing hard, he pulled on the scarlet coronation robe. It slipped down over his body, fitting perfectly. He looked down at his hands. They were shaking.

He twisted his father's ring, but instead of comfort he felt a fresh wave of shame. All he could think of was how little he deserved to wear it. Better to take it off. He slipped it free and left it on the bed. He busied himself putting on the rest of the regalia: the gold chain of office, the belt, the pectorals. Then he rejoined Tyrus outside.

All too soon, he was in the curtained-off antechamber. The sound of hundreds of voices drifted through from the main hall, a low babble of anxious conversation. A fanfare sounded, and the voices hushed. Gentle hands were at his back, ushering him forward.

No backing out now, he thought to himself, smoothing down his front. He swallowed again; his throat was dry. *Let's get this over with*.

He stepped through the curtains.

3

Ayl caught Keller's eye as he sat down. The Aquanth expected him to wink, but he didn't.

Ayl felt dry and hot in his ceremonial robe. He desperately wanted a deep, cool breath of water; his gills were starting to crust. It wasn't just the heat in the chamber, or the hushed expectation as everyone waited for the ceremony finally to begin. It was the sense of panic thumping and growing inside him.

Something terrible was going to happen. He shut his eyes. In his mind's eye he saw the future like a massive wave of dark water, cold and impossible to outrun, rushing towards them all from the horizon. Nobody else could see it. Only him.

Ayl gave an involuntary hiss of warning, which sounded loud in the silent hall. His mother gave him a worried look. He shook his head and turned away.

The Aquanth forced himself to look around the room. The seats were filled with a shoal of brightly coloured figures, dignitaries and ambassadors from across the galaxy. Every one, from the towering bark-skinned Arborials to the squat, pig-nosed Ogrics, wore a long robe that brushed the floor. No matter how ridiculous they looked, they were honouring tradition.

Nothing sinister stood out from the crowd. Even so, Ayl knew something bad was going to happen. The black wave was very close now. It was gathering momentum, blotting out the sky, and soon it would come crashing down upon them all.

Some grey-bearded Cantorian was giving an opening address. Ayl barely registered the words. The whole room felt like it was going to implode. Unable to bear it any longer, he linked minds with his mother. *We have to stop the coronation!* he raged silently. *There's a threat – I just know there is!*

Her voice in his mind was strong and steady. *Be calm.* And then a lesser but longer thought, like a mighty backwash: *There is no threat here. The Nara-Karith were destroyed. The Bellori are on guard – try to enjoy your friend's big day.*

Ayl glanced over at Dray, realising he was afraid for her too. *They don't know. We have to warn them!*

He focused his mind on Dray, trying to send a warning message to her. But his thoughts spattered like raindrops on her mind, unable to penetrate. She was too deep in her own thoughts to notice his.

His mother's next thoughts flashed into his mind like reflected moonlight on a lapping sea. *Ayl, this is an occasion of peace. Everyone present here is an ally.*

Faster than an anemone's tendrils vanishing back into its body, Ayl withdrew his thoughts into his own mind.

The talks on the asteroid were an occasion of peace too, he thought ruefully to himself. *Everyone present was an ally. And what happened? The Nara-Karith attacked, and nearly tore our system apart!*

Beside him, his mother stood to speak out loud. 'In the name of the One Current of Life that unites us all, flowing through our hearts and minds, bearing us ever onward to further evolution and deeper understanding . . .' Her voice sounded so strange and small when it wasn't echoing inside his head. '. . . we bless this coronation, and offer our prayers for the new trade king. May wisdom guide him to rule in peace and harmony.'

There was a rumble of assent from the assembled guests.

Her voice softened. 'The wise have often said that destiny may bring joy and sorrow on the same tide. As we celebrate the new trade king, let us remember the last. Trade King Lial died heroically, and his sacrifice opened the way for a new future of peace. I ask you all to join with me in a moment's silence to honour his memory, after which we will join in the *Hamrith-Kha*, the chant of homecoming.'

Somewhat awkwardly, with a lot of shuffling, the guests bowed their heads. Ayl did the same. He tried to think kindly of Trade King Lial. An image of the man's face came into his mind, but his eyes were lifeless and staring. A stream of blood was flowing from his mouth. A ragged wound gaped in his chest, and the Nara-Karith were chittering nearby.

None of these silent guests had seen it happen. Ayl had. Keller's father had died in front of him, a victim of the Nara-Karith. The nightmare wouldn't end. The Nara-Karith seemed to be piling into his skull, scuttling and scraping inside his brain. He strained to push the memories out.

'*Kha ne mo ra ghol a ne. Kha ne mo ra ghol a ne.*' His mother's voice, clear and powerful now, led the chant. There was no definitive translation from the ancient Aquanth, but it roughly meant, 'Let the one who bore life return safely to the source of life.'

He raised his voice to join the chant. He didn't even

care about the meaning. He just wanted the noise to drown out those memories.

Dray narrowed her eyes. Fish-boy looked like he was going to start gasping and flopping on the floor.

Must be the heat. She felt a trickle of sweat run down her back inside her armour plates, but kept still and alert. She had a job to do and she was going to do it properly. She was Bellori, she told herself; she could stay standing with a dozen knife wounds in her, so what was a stifling hot throne room?

She carried out a threat assessment, her gaze resting for a moment on one guest then flicking on to the next. The deep blue dwarf-like creatures with the curved tusks and spiral tattoos looked alarming in their bone-adorned robes, but she knew they were Pozliks, the most docile species imaginable unless their burrows were threatened.

Pious and pale, the huge-eyed Oholoo were chanting with gusto, but there could easily be room for a blaster under those white robes. The squid-headed Vraal, black-robed like mourners, had a history of assassination and treachery, but only among their own kind. She moved on.

After far too long, the Aquanth chant finished. Still

40

more ceremony to endure, though. Keller sat stock still on his throne as a document was presented to him.

'The Treaty of Callifrax, binding the king to uphold free trade!' boomed a bearded Cantorian official. 'Let it be signed!'

It was signed.

'Bring forth the samthorn wine and the falchort egg!' the official said.

They were brought in on a quantanium tray carried between two servants.

Dray curled her lip in contempt. *Cantorians.* Everything they did, they overdid. On Bellus, this would have been over already.

Keller raised the golden goblet of samthorn wine, which the official proclaimed was 'The wealth of Cantor', and drained it. Dray froze, watching for signs of poison, but Keller seemed none the worse. The green falchort egg symbolized 'The fertility of Cantor'. Keller ate it, chewing in absolute silence.

Dray had to admit that not everybody could make eating an egg into a solemn occasion and carry it off. Keller certainly looked royal, his golden regalia gleaming in the sun. What must it be like, to be king of a whole world at his age? To be responsible for so many, entrusted with so much?

Robed officials moved around Keller's throne as if they were orbiting his sun, carrying away the ritual implements, bringing new ones. Locked inside her armour, unseen, unnoticed, Dray craved that recognition.

One day, she swore, people would look at her and know who she was, what she had done. She would be hidden away like an embarrassment no more. She would have authority, just like Keller did, and what was more, she would *earn* it.

Just let the opportunity come. Then she would prove herself.

She would be ready.

Keller's right buttock had gone numb. The throne had been built for splendour, not comfort, and the ancient jungawood was like granite.

Slowly, so as not to be too obvious, he shifted his weight on to the other cheek. Had anyone noticed? Impossible to tell, since everyone was looking at him anyway.

His face felt hot and flushed. The collar of his robe was chafing. A bead of sweat rolled down and hung in one eyebrow.

'We proceed to the Recitation of the Lineage!' Tyrus announced.

The heat was bad enough, but Keller's head was swimming now from gulping down a whole goblet of samthorn wine. It burned like liquid gingery gold in his throat. He burped, tasted egg, and managed to make it look like a cough.

'Lorux the First, named Lorux the Resplendent, builder of the Imperial Exchange,' droned Tyrus. 'Succeeded by Brantis of Wen, named Brantis the Huge, on account of his stature . . .'

Keller groaned inwardly. Tyrus was going to recite the names and titles of every single trade king of Cantor. It was like slow torture.

Surely there couldn't be much more of this to go. Keller focused his mind on the feast to come. Food. More wine. Dancing in huge air-conditioned halls. Maybe he and some friends could cut loose and have a private party in the upper galleries, or even break out the Mazakomi and go racing! There were old scores to settle . . .

No. He cut his thoughts off sharply. He was about to become a king. That meant behaving with dignity. No more lectures from Tyrus.

'Vorn Forkbeard, named Vorn Tightfist, for his excessive taxation . . .'

The list went on and on. Much like the days in front

of him, really. Keller began to feel the full burden of his position weigh down on him. There would be no wild parties again, ever. He was a representative of all Cantor now.

Instead, there would be audiences, state occasions, hearings. Piles of admin and officials tugging at his sleeves. It was as if he was being sent back to school, forever.

He looked up past the assembled alien guests to the upper galleries, where crowds of local Cantorians had gathered. He got a shock. All their faces were stony, their eyes sharp. Wasn't this meant to be a happy occasion?

He looked for a single smile, a single kind expression. There were none. Many of the Cantorians even looked as if they would gladly spit on him.

Maybe they were just bored by the recitation. That had to be it. Keller hoped he was being paranoid, but in his heart he was sure they despised him.

I'm sorry, he thought miserably. *I know how much you loved my father. I can't hope to replace him. I'll be a disappointment, I just know I will.*

Trumpets blared a triumphant fanfare, in stark opposition to Keller's dark thoughts. He was suddenly aware that Tyrus was no longer speaking.

His moment had come at last.

Keller stood up and knelt down in front of the throne. He saw Tyrus raise the Crown of Cantor, three flawless natural diamonds blazing from the brow.

He closed his eyes, waiting for the touch of cold metal on his head.

And the sound of gunshots ripped through the silence.

Dray was already moving. Everyone else had heard the shot. Only Dray had heard the telltale click of a safety lock being removed, a split second before.

One chance, if she was fast enough.

She threw herself through the air, turning as she went, trying to cover as much of Keller's body with her own as she could. Three hard shots like power hammers slammed into her, cracking her armour, sending her spinning backwards into Keller.

She landed on top of him and fell sprawling.

Even with the protection of keratin plates, gouts of pain were searing her chest. She wheezed for breath. It *hurt*. She could taste blood.

No time for that now. *Find the enemy. Kill him.*

Around her, the throne room erupted in panic. Screams rang out and the guests flooded towards the exits. Ogrics squealed like pigs, and the Vraal were spraying black ink in their fear, drenching bystanders.

'Secure the exits!' Iccus yelled, forming a one-man barricade on the stairs. 'Don't let the assassin escape!' The other Bellori sprang to obey.

Dray scrambled to her feet, panting hard.

The Bellori were blocking the doors as best they could, but she could already tell it was far too late. Whoever the assassin was, they had been well prepared. They would be making their escape by now.

Her father hadn't even looked in her direction. She decided to feel proud about that. If he'd worried about her, it would have meant he thought she was weak.

She remembered Keller. He hadn't yelled when she landed on him. He hadn't said *anything*.

Dray looked into his face. He had closed his eyes as the crown came down. She realized he had not opened them again.

'Help me carry him!' she barked to another Bellori.

Together they dragged Keller into the curtained preparation room. He felt heavy and limp.

Dead weight.

4

The black wave of terror came thundering down on Ayl, crushing him with its force. He was helpless as a newtling.

I can't stop this, I can't help them, it's happening now, the death, the death again . . .

Ayl clutched his head, reeling, the sound of gunshots still ringing inside his brain. Those three sharp ugly blasts hauled him back to the asteroid, back to the Nara-Karith, back to the killing and the blood. He was trapped again, cast into a world of violent hate.

Dray and Keller had been there too, on the asteroid. He could almost consider them friends. But Ayl didn't even look up to see if Keller was still alive. He buried his face in his hands, repeating 'No, no, no . . .'

His mother was there, immediately, holding him. 'Be calm, Ayl!'

He threw her off. 'Blood. Everywhere.' He struggled

to explain through the riot in his head. 'They're killing the trade king . . .'

Lady Moa grabbed his arm. 'Hush. The Bellori are here. They are on alert, the area is secure, we are safe. You must calm yourself, try to—'

'It's too late!' Ayl snapped back into focus as he saw Dray hauling Keller's limp body into the next room. 'I knew something bad was going to happen. I tried to warn you!'

'Ayl . . .'

'You didn't listen!'

His mother, left without a reply for once, sat open-mouthed.

In a sudden spasm of anger, Ayl stood and walked away. A few paces on, he hesitated and turned around. There was something he had to say.

'They're back,' he said slowly. 'The Nara-Karith. I can feel them . . . sense them. They did this.'

'You carry a heavy burden in your heart, my son, and it is making you irrational,' his mother said carefully. 'I take the blame. You should have remained on Aquanthis and received healing. I should not have brought you here.'

'Irrational?' Ayl yelled, no longer caring who might hear. 'You saw what happened! They've come for Keller just like they murdered his father! It's *them*!'

Link minds with me, his mother thought urgently to him.

Reluctantly, Ayl interwove his mind with hers.

Together, they shared his mother's memories from a minute before. Through her eyes, Ayl saw Keller kneel and Tyrus raise the crown. Then, in the back row of the audience, a humanoid figure stepped into the aisle and raised a long rifle. It wore a purple robe, hooded, with broad sleeves. No face could be seen.

The rifle's muzzle flashed three times, and Ayl winced each time as if he was being shot himself.

Do you see? The assassin was no Nara-Karith, his mother thought to him. *It was humanoid, like us. The Nara-Karith were like gigantic spiders.*

Ayl began to think about Bellori military technology, and how a Nara-Karith might have cloaked itself, but his mother caught the thought.

Not even a holo-net could have disguised a beast of that size, she told him. *There are no Nara-Karith here. All of them were destroyed. They exist only in your memories.*

'I don't know *how* I know!' Ayl insisted, speaking aloud again in his frustration. 'Don't ask me to explain! The Nara-Karith are involved in this, somehow. There's a connection. If I could just . . . I don't . . .'

His mother was firm. *That is your fear and your guilt talking. Be here now, Ayl. Our allies will need us.*

Keller opened his eyes. Dray was standing over him, holding a vase of Vashtali midnight blooms, about to empty the water over his head. A semicircle of concerned onlookers had filtered in from the throne room and were watching.

'Whoa!' he shouted, sitting up. 'Put the vase down and back away. I'm fine.'

A twinge of pain from his back made him wince, and he sank back to the floor. He rolled on to his side like a reclining statue, propping himself on one elbow and grinning up at Dray.

'You make a very convincing corpse,' Dray said icily.

'Thanks!' Keller said. 'And . . . thanks. Seriously. For saving my life.'

Dray gave a curt nod.

'Sorry if I scared you there,' Keller said. 'I figured I'd better keep my eyes shut and play dead. In case—'

'In case the assassin realized he'd failed to kill you? I don't think he stayed in the room that long. You're bleeding.'

Keller examined his elbow. 'Just a scratch.'

'Anything else damaged?'

Keller shrugged. It hurt, but he just said, 'Few bruises. That armour's heavy.'

Dray didn't bother with a spoken response. She jabbed a thumb at the three deep indentations in her armour. Keller understood. The Bellori plate was heavy for good reason. It could stop a laser-guided high-impact bullet. Or three.

The sight of the bullet marks made Keller feel queasy and faint. If just one had hit him, they'd have had to clean him off the floor with a pressure hose.

Who on earth would want to assassinate a trade king? He thought of all the strange alien races gathered in the throne room and wondered what private grievances they might have. Could any of them hate Cantor that much? Surely Cantor had brought them nothing but prosperity.

Then he remembered the rows and rows of stony Cantorian faces staring down at him. Any one of them could easily have hidden a blaster under those heavy robes.

Of course, the guards were meant to search people for hidden weapons, but the guards were Cantorians too. And the officials, and the serving staff.

No wonder they despised him, he thought glumly.

He wasn't a fit heir to the throne. He knew it, and his people knew it. Obviously, someone thought he should be removed right away, for Cantor's sake.

No point in trying to guess who. It was harder to think of a Cantorian who *didn't* have reason to hate him.

Keller checked himself. He was getting paranoid. It was probably some lone noble with a grudge, wanting a son from his own line on the throne. There was more than enough of that sort of skulduggery in Cantor's past.

There was blood on his rich brocade robes. Dray was looking at it, and at him.

He got to his feet, made a big show of dusting himself down, and helped himself to some more Samthorn wine. He held out the goblet to Dray, and when she did nothing, shrugged and drained it.

'Here's to the life of a trade king!' he said, smacking his lips. 'Glory, honour and prestige! I knew girls would soon be throwing themselves at me. I just didn't expect a Bellori to be the first.'

'This isn't a time to make jokes, Keller,' said Dray.

'On the contrary. I think it's a perfect time. I'm still alive, thanks to you, and I intend to celebrate. Cheers.'

Dray folded her arms. 'Fine. While you're having fun, think about this: how did you manage to make an enemy before you were even crowned?'

Keller froze, with the cup halfway to his mouth. He felt the colour drain from his face. Dray's words had hit him like a blow to the stomach.

He wasn't the new trade king at all. The crown had never reached his head.

They hadn't wanted to give him even a *chance* at ruling Cantor. The thought sickened him and excited him at the same time. He was still free . . .

The future that had seemed so dreary and rock-solid had smashed into a trillion fragments. His mind raced frantically. What if he just wasn't meant to be king? What if his destiny was something different altogether? If the people didn't want him, and he didn't want the job anyway, perhaps being shot at might be the best thing that had happened to him all day.

It could work. He could use this!

His keen bargaining mind was already working out the details. If he played this right, he could just disappear from the scene. Let someone else have the duty and the responsibility.

He looked out of the window at the blue sky. Suddenly it didn't seem so far away any more.

* * *

Iccus barged through the onlookers and joined Dray and Keller at the window. Keller looked at him warily, like a cadet caught just as he was about to do something he shouldn't. Dray thought he looked shifty all of a sudden.

'He's alive,' Dray said, nodding in Keller's direction.

'So I see,' said Iccus, tapping her damaged chest plate. 'Excellent work.'

Dray hadn't expected praise. 'Thank you, sir.'

'You thought fast and, more importantly, you moved fast. I see you've not been lying to me about your extra hours of training.'

'I only acted as any true Bellori would act,' Dray said, fighting to keep her voice at a controlled level. At last her father had noticed her abilities. The sense of triumph she was feeling threatened to break out of her in a war whoop.

Iccus waved a dismissive hand. 'Enough modesty. I have been thinking, Dray. I have come to a decision concerning your future.'

'Sir?'

'I think we may have been . . . *over-hasty* in wishing to keep you away from combat. You have talents. Talents that should be used, not left to rust.'

He paused, looking Dray up and down as if he were assessing her.

Dray stood to attention, every muscle tense. *Get to the point, Father!*

'I have created an official role for you.'

Inside her helmet, Dray silently mouthed the word *Yes*.

'It is what you deserve, my daughter. Your swift actions in the throne room have proved that, once and for all.'

Dray clenched her fist, brimming over with excitement. At last her father was recognising her bravery. This was her moment, and it had been a long time coming. Well, better late than never.

Iccus began to pace up and down. 'Today's events are likely to be just the beginning. We cannot dismiss them as a one-off. Cantor's new king clearly has enemies, *powerful* enemies, and as the only warriors of the Trinity System, it is our duty to address that threat.'

The assassin! He had to be talking about hunting the assassin down.

Dray imagined herself leading a troop of hand-picked elite warriors, tracking the assassin to his lair, setting herself up in a sniper's nest, getting him in her sights . . . no, a kill from a distance would be too impersonal. Better to confront him one-on-one, blade in hand . . .

'You will therefore enter the service of Cantor immediately,' Iccus said. 'As Trade Prince Keller's personal bodyguard.'

5

Ayl stood alone in the splendid royal bathrooms, splashing cold water on his face. It flowed from golden taps shaped like Aquanth krakens. Dignity be damned. He had to feel water on his skin. Any water.

He stared at his reflection, willing himself to be calm.

I need to get control of myself. I have abilities, so I should use them. Think! What should an Aquanth do when he feels panic?

Perhaps he needed more than just water. He needed to immerse himself in the healing soul of Aquanthis itself. He would mind-link with his circle of friends, the people he'd known since childhood. Har, Sef, Lok, Chel and Wan . . . surely Wan wouldn't reject him again, now there was no solemn naptarch watching over them?

Ayl concentrated, focusing his mind on his homeworld. Though it was far away, he felt the link forming in an instant.

The image of the blue planet loomed large in his mind, millions of Aquanth minds shining like bright beacons, as if to welcome him home. He felt the darkness and terror falling away from him like a shroud.

His friends were gathered outside the Caverns of Study, snacking on kelp and laughing together like they'd done with him a thousand times. Ayl merged his thoughts with theirs. Like a drop of rain flowing into the ocean, he let himself become part of the group. At last, peace.

It only lasted a few clicks. He felt the combined force of their minds rejecting him, trying to force him out.

Ayl! Get out! bellowed Sef. *You'll pollute us all!*

I saw inside his mind, said little Chel, shuddering. *It's horrible.*

Guys, it's me! Ayl pleaded, struggling desperately to stay linked to the group. *I haven't changed, just let me stay with you for a moment, you'll understand . . .*

Lok's thoughts were like spears of ice. *How dare you bring such thoughts to us? We are pure! The violence in your memories will damage us! Get out!*

It was even worse than what had happened at the temple. A naptarch warning people not to link with him was one thing, but how could his friends turn on him like this?

Wan, tell them! he insisted. *Tell them it's me! I'm not dangerous!*

Wan's thoughts were grave. *I'm sorry, Ayl. I don't recognize you any more. You shouldn't have tried to come back.*

Then he was flung back, sent spinning through mind-space away from Aquanthis. He saw how his friends had seen him – a dark drop of blood, not water, staining their peaceful clarity with murk and filth.

Ayl stood up, slowly.

He left the bathrooms and worked his way across the throne room to the curtained antechamber where Keller had been dragged. The room was filling up with diplomats and hangers-on.

To his amazement, both Keller and Dray were still alive. They turned to see him approach, and Keller grinned in welcome. Ayl felt such joy and relief to see them he could have shouted out loud.

That settles it, he thought. *This is where I belong.*

He crossed the room to where his mother stood. If she had any idea of what had just happened on Aquanthis, it did not show on her face.

'Mother?'

'Yes, Ayl?'

'I won't be returning to Aquanthis with you. I want to stay here on Cantor.'

She looked pained. 'Ayl. I know you have been upset, deeply upset, but now is when you most need to stand beside your people—'

'No,' he said coldly, shocking her into silence. 'What's the point? Everything that happened on the asteroid, and now this. It's part of me now, in my memory, forever. I'm *different* now.'

'Your memories will fade in time.'

'My people, you say? I'm disgusting to them. An outcast! How can I go back now?' He thought of Wan, and pain cut through him like a blade. 'Who would want to link minds with a . . . a tainted freak?'

'I would,' she said softly. 'You could never be anything but good and true in my eyes, my child. Whatever help you need, I will give it.'

It was almost enough to change his mind. Then he glanced at Dray and Keller again.

'I have friends here. They need me,' he said. 'And I need them. I need people who *listen*.'

His mother shook her head. 'You are not responsible for what happened to you in the past, Ayl. You must learn to live with that darkness in your own way. But I warn you now, if you turn away from your people, you turn your back on who you are. Do that at your peril!'

' "We stand united as one"?' Ayl quoted, the words bitter on his tongue now.

'Aquanths do not seek to be selfish individuals like members of other races. Our strength is in our unity.'

'I've heard that a thousand times, Mother. I'm a little sick of it.'

'Very well. Turn away from me if you must. But the strength of Aquanth unity is real. Don't cut yourself off from it, Ayl, or when you need it most it will not be there for you.'

There was a long pause. She held out her hand to him.

He took it and looked deep into her pleading eyes.

'I'm staying here on Cantor,' Ayl said. 'And that's final.'

Dray was furious.

She flipped the display inside her helmet from setting to setting: normal, infrared, hi-viz, vector-enhanced. It gave her something to do while she was stuck here on the sidelines, watching over her new charge.

Keller's heat silhouette looked like a flaming purple

mass. *Click*. Now he was a wire-frame model, with the most deadly spots to strike at marked on his body. *Click*. Now he was a teenager in a robe again, smirking at some private joke of his own.

'Everyone here that ought to be?' demanded Tyrus. 'Right. The situation is urgent and we need to act now. General Iccus, what are your thoughts?'

'You're lucky to be alive,' Iccus snapped. 'All of you. We know this much, at least. Whoever the assassin was, he was picky about his target. If he'd thrown a bomb, or even a frag-grenade, you'd be dripping from the ceiling right now.'

'That's not helpful,' said Lady Moa. 'We need to stay calm. Let us try to remember exactly what happened.'

As her father began to pick over the events leading up to the shooting, Dray kept up her resentful glaring at Keller.

'Don't blame *me*,' Keller eventually hissed at her. 'It wasn't my idea to make you my new guard dog. I've got enough hunting hounds already.'

'Hunting's what I *want* to do!' whispered Dray. 'I ought to be tracking the assassin. It makes more sense than watching over you.'

'I nearly got killed!'

'And how likely is it that they'll try again, with the

whole palace on high-alert?'

Keller looked amused. 'You want to go hunting for an assassin? Fine by me. I've seen what you can do.'

Dray approached Iccus, who was watching Tyrus and the high priestess argue over which worlds might have sneaked an assassin into the hall. Behind them, the Oholoo and the Vraal delegations looked like they were about to start fighting. All around, the noise of bickering voices was growing louder.

'Father?'

'I know what you are going to ask,' said Iccus. 'The answer is no.'

'But this is a waste of my abilities! I'm trained for much more than just guard duty! Keller says—'

'Leave the job of tracking the assassin to the experienced warriors, Dray,' Iccus said. 'You have your assignment. Attend to it.'

He strode across the room and forcibly separated the Oholoo and Vraal ambassadors. Dray watched him, silently fuming.

'Order!' Iccus bellowed, slamming his fist on a table. The racket simmered down to a quiet murmur. 'I will not let this occasion collapse into chaos!' he continued, his visor glowing an ominous red. 'That is what the enemy wants!'

'While we do not yet know who the assassin is,' piped up an Aquanth, 'we cannot guess at what he – or she – might want.'

'Then that should be our first concern,' a Cantorian said. 'Who tried to assassinate our new trade king?'

'They wore purple – the colour of the Yaanok merchant house of Cantor!' rasped one of the Bellori guard.

'The assassin's clothing doesn't matter,' spluttered another of the Aquanths. 'What matters is who he was working for!'

The room erupted into a flurry of suggestions. Iccus had to bang the table for silence again.

Then Lady Moa's clear voice declared, 'We can be certain who the assassin was *not*. They were not one of the races from beyond the Trinity System. They were humanoid, like us.'

'Yes. They must have come from one of our three worlds,' agreed Iccus.

'Most likely a Cantorian trader,' said Tyrus. 'Someone with a good reason to hate young Keller here. Let's face it, his business dealings haven't all been on the level, have they?'

'You put an attempted assassination down to a *personal grudge*?' said a horrified Aquanth. 'That is absurd!'

'Surely an attack on Cantorian royalty is an act of war,' commented a Bellorian.

'It may very well be,' said Iccus. 'That decides us. I will give the order to set up a Bellori army base on Cantor, so that we can protect you, our allies. Tyrus, make the necessary arrangements for billeting and supply.'

While Tyrus blustered, the high priestess stepped forward. 'We are *not* decided. Far from it! Military action would be sorely premature at this point. What we must do now is pray.'

'Pray, Lady Moa?' Iccus mocked. 'So the enemy can find us kneeling, all the better to offer our surrender?'

'We must pray for a peaceful resolution!' the priestess said in a voice of ice.

'What about Keller?' Dray cut in. 'How long am I supposed to babysit him?'

Tyrus sniffed. 'We should move him to a safe house, for his own protection. That way, we'll know exactly where he is and what he's doing.'

'Agreed,' said Iccus.

Even the high priestess nodded.

Great, thought Dray. *Locked up behind the walls of a safe house. Nothing gets in or out. Not even the prospect of a fight to look forward to.*

* * *

Keller had heard enough. He took a deep breath and spoke up. 'Thank you all for your suggestions, and your offers of help,' he began. 'We value your allegiance, every one of you. But I'm going to ask you all to leave now. This is a Cantorian matter. We can deal with it by ourselves. Thank you. Goodbye.'

Nobody left. Nobody even paid him the slightest attention.

'Tyrus?' Keller tugged at the man's sleeve. 'Back me up, would you? I am the one in charge here.'

Tyrus was deep in discussion with Iccus. Something about safe house wall thickness and defence turrets. He barely spared Keller a glance.

Keller sat down in a slump, thinking of what awaited him now.

He had been inside the royal safe house once before, during a safety drill. It was a high-security bunker buried under the planet's surface. There was nothing to do but watch old vids and eat bland, preserved food. It was like prison.

But . . . he *would* be safe in there. There would be games and simulators to play with. He wouldn't have those clear blue skies, but holo-fields inside fake windows would make it *look* like he did. They could replicate any scene from the outside world. He could put his feet up, stop worrying so much. Other people would handle all the work and the politics. It could almost be like a holiday. He'd have Dray's company too. She wasn't bad for a Bellori, not once you got to know her . . .

He looked her way, saw her standing tensely on guard, and thought: *What on Cantor am I thinking? That girl's like a wild thrattacat! Cooped up with one another in a plascrete box under the ground? We'll go out of our minds!*

'I don't think so,' he muttered to himself.

He motioned for Dray to follow him, then crossed the room to where Ayl was standing alone.

'Come on, you two,' he said. 'Follow me. We're leaving.'

'Are you sure?' Ayl said. 'Shouldn't we at least say where we're—'

Keller grabbed him by one clammy arm and led him out of the room. 'Just keep walking.'

As they left the room, Keller quickly glanced back. Nobody had noticed them leave. All the people in the room were clustered around Tyrus, Iccus and the high priestess, still deep in discussion.

'Quick,' Keller said. 'Up these stairs to the gallery,

then along to the amber room. Before anyone notices we've gone.'

Dray's heavy boots thumped on the marble floor. Ayl, gasping, struggled to keep up. They reached the next floor, then followed Keller through a jewel-encrusted room to a service lift.

'Where are you taking us?' Dray groused as she squeezed herself inside.

'You'll see,' replied Keller.

His finger stabbed the lift button, and the doors slid shut.

6

'This is your royal bedchamber?' Dray said, as Keller unlocked the door.

'Yeah,' said Keller. 'I don't usually let anyone else in here, but under the circumstances . . .'

He opened the door. Dray glanced in and stopped him before he could enter, blocking the door with her arm. 'Don't move!'

'What's wrong?'

'It's been ransacked. Someone's turned the place upside down.' She nodded at the scene of chaos inside the room.

Piles of clothes were strewn about, cabinets lay open, drawers hung where they had been pulled. An entertainment centre was all but unrecognisable under piles of data slates and game cartridges. Portable computers, gadgets, plasma doodlers, odd socks, zero-gee sports gear and holo-comix littered the floor. The room's contents had been flung every which way without care or attention.

'That's one seriously messed-up room,' said Ayl.

'Whoever did this must have been searching for something,' Dray said excitedly. Despite her father's wishes, she was on the assassin's trail after all. Maybe he was even inside the room. She braced herself for a fight.

'But . . .'

'It's got to be connected to the shooting! Think, Keller! What were they looking for, and did they find it?'

Keller sighed heavily. 'Dray, would you just listen? Nobody's been in here but me. It always looks like this.'

Dray very badly wanted to tell Keller exactly what she thought of him then, but stopped herself. She was his bodyguard now. Bodyguards weren't meant to insult their charges. So instead, she thought about how hard she'd landed on him before, and felt satisfied.

'Thought you had servants to clean up after you?' Ayl said with bemusement.

'They're not allowed in here. Nobody is unless I say so. Come on.'

Dray followed him into the room. 'Mind where you step,' Keller warned. 'I don't want you breaking any of my stuff.'

As if on cue, Dray heard a sharp *crack* from under

70

her boot. Keller winced but said nothing. He went and stroked the head of a crimson hunting hound that lay curled up in a pet bed – a bed more plush and fancy than any Bellori would sleep in, let alone their pet. The hound stirred, licked Keller's hand, then went back to sleep.

Dray scowled in disgust and turned away to look at the walls. *That thing's so pampered it's forgotten it's an animal. Predators are supposed to hunt.*

The walls were hung with holographic images of Keller: here was Keller beside his father, looking stern and majestic; here he was in the cockpit of some flashy racing ship; here he was again in what must have been a magazine's fashion section, wearing a tight-fitting green and white sports suit.

The real Keller was moodily selecting a song on a data slate, filling the room with a thumping beat. He was noticeably chubbier than the images on the wall, Dray thought. He was getting a double chin.

One part of the room, clearer than the rest, held a tall glass cabinet. On transparent racks stood trophies in chrome and silver with engraved bases. *FIRST PLACE – Cassibo Light-Engine Tournament*, Dray read. *FIRST PLACE – Wambah Three-Day Burn-off*. A scale model of the flashy racing ship stood among the cups, rotating slowly in a small forcefield.

Keller and Ayl had sat down, so Dray decided to join them. She shoved a heap of clutter off the bed, brushed off a matted layer of hound hair and sat. The soft bed all but engulfed her.

There was something shiny lying on the bed. A ring.

Keller saw her looking. He quickly snatched up the ring and put it on.

'What's that?' Dray asked.

'It was my father's,' Keller said with a glare.

Dray didn't waste time wondering what his problem was. There were more important things to concern herself with, like the state of her armour. A Bellori who didn't check her armour regularly would end up dead sooner or later.

She carefully inspected her chest plate, running a gloved finger over the edges of each deep impact point, probing them for depth. Bellori armour was made of dozens of sandwiched layers, fused into a mesh stronger than a spaceship's hull. None of the bullets had come close to full penetration. At most, they were a third of the way through the thick plating.

'Let's see what we're dealing with,' she muttered. Ayl and Keller watched silently as she unsheathed her *scratha* knife and dug the point around inside one of the holes, hunting for the bullet. 'Come out, you wretched thing . . .'

'Careful!' Ayl said.

Dray shook her head. As if she was in danger of hurting herself!

She levered the blade, using both hands for extra force, and a crushed metal wad popped out and skittered over the floor. 'Got it!'

'What is it?' asked Keller.

She held the bullet between thumb and forefinger. 'From the shape, it's a bullet from a k-gun. A Bellori model, like the ones our military use.'

'I thought *all* Bellori were military,' pondered Ayl.

Keller looked wary. 'So the shooter was one of your people?'

'Sorry. It's not Bellori manufacture. Wrong sort of metal.'

'Well, it's a clue, at least!' Keller said. 'Right now, it's our *only* clue. Maybe I can check the library, or find a scanner and run some tests . . .'

Dray stood up. 'Let me worry about finding the assassin, Keller. I'm going to be your bodyguard from here on in. Get used to it.'

* * *

73

I don't need a bodyguard!' Keller scoffed, hating the idea. 'And if I did, I'd hire a battle droid or a Rhondrian hornbeast, not you!' He paused. 'Nothing personal.'

'If people are shooting at you, which they are, then you do need a bodyguard,' Dray said drily. 'Anyway, it doesn't matter what you or I think. We're stuck with each other.'

Her matter-of-fact tone was infuriating. Keller wasn't taking that. 'I'm heir to the throne of Cantor. Nobody tells me what I can and can't do!'

'And I am Bellori!' Dray retorted sharply. 'My father gave me an order, and we Bellori follow our orders!'

'Hey! Give it a rest!' said Ayl. 'You want to cool it down with all this bickering and point scoring? Sometimes, you're as bad as our parents.'

He's right, thought Keller. *Fish-boy's got a point.*

'Whatever,' Keller said. 'I guess I don't have a choice about it any more than Dray does. We'd better start working as a team to figure this out.'

'That's the most sensible thing you've said all morning,' Dray muttered.

'Step one is to get us out of this place,' Keller said. 'Listen. I've got a plan . . .'

Moments later, they were sneaking along the corridor away from Keller's room. Music was still pumping from

74

behind the door, turned up extra loud. Keller let Dray scout ahead, in case any guards were waiting for them.

Dray pressed herself against the wall next to a featureless white door. 'In here?'

Keller nodded. They burst in, and he hit the lights. They were standing inside a store cupboard, where freshly pressed uniforms lay in rows on airing shelves. They were colour coded, Keller explained: white for domestic staff; blue for maintenance and engineering; yellow for sanitation; and so on.

'Ah!' said Ayl, stepping into a white laundry porter's uniform. 'Clever. I'm still too blue to pass for a Cantorian, though.'

'I thought of that.' Keller passed him a jar of Insta-Tan cream. 'Rub that on. The nanoparticles layer over your natural skin colour.'

'Make-up, Keller?' said Dray. 'I should have known.'

'For photo shoots!' Keller said defensively. He struggled into a uniform of his own. 'How do I look?' he asked, buttoning up the tight-fitting front.

Ayl cocked his head. 'Actually, it suits you.'

'It's more comfortable than my coronation robes, anyway!' Keller laughed.

Dray didn't join in the laughter. She stood to one side, arms folded, like a security robot in guard mode.

'You too, Dray,' Keller said, holding up a maid's uniform. It had a pinafore.

'The sun's core will be a cold dead lump of ash before I get into that!' Dray hissed.

'We've got to be inconspicuous,' Keller said, doing his best to be patient with her. 'Two kitchen staff and a Bellori warrior doesn't make sense!'

'I know. I *have* studied camouflage.'

'Come on. At least we'll all look stupid together.'

'It's not that,' Dray said. 'I'll have to leave my armour behind. Don't pretend you don't know what that means to me.'

'Yeah, I do know,' Keller said quietly. 'But, Dray — we need you to do this. I promise you, your armour will be safe.'

'I'm holding you to that.' She reached up and twisted her helmet, lifted it off and shook her hair loose. For an instant, Keller caught himself looking into her eyes — her real eyes, pale and bright in her lean face. Then the armour plates were sliding and folding like a conjuring trick, and she was climbing out of the suit.

Keller gaped. Out of her armour, she looked so small, so vulnerable.

'No need to stare,' Dray snapped at him.

76

'Nothing I haven't seen before,' Keller retorted.

Dray ignored the maid's outfit Keller had offered and pulled on a yellow boiler suit instead, then turned back to her armour. She tugged a module free from her forearm guard and with a few twists and clicks, it became a snub-nosed pistol. With the press of a toggle, a flat disc from her kneepad became a throwing star. The grooved front of her shinguard was a lean knife blade. Keller was amazed. It was as if her armour was made entirely of concealed weapons.

In a few clicks, they were concealed once again as Dray tucked them into the folds of her uniform.

'So,' she asked. 'What's the best way out of here?"

Ayl's skin felt drier than ever under the layer of Insta-Tan, but at least he looked much like any other Cantorian now. The three of them kept their heads down as they walked down the palace corridors, holding piles of linen in front of them. Ayl watched Dray's feet, using them as a guide for where to walk. If he turned his head too far, his gill slits would open.

He had to admit he was excited. It was good to be back with Dray and Keller again, doing crazy, dangerous, *unique* things. As they crossed a windowed walkway linking two sections of the palace, Ayl saw the manta-like shape of the Aquanth flagship lift gracefully over the buildings.

His mother would be inside, heading back to Aquanthis without him. Suddenly she was there, inside his mind, her thoughts feeding into his own in a swell of sorrow:

Be careful, my only son. Choose well who you trust. I will pray for you.

She did not remain mind-linked for long enough to receive his answer. The graceful ship was soaring away, vanishing beyond the clouds.

Ayl felt a pang like a sliver of bone in his heart. It gave him no pleasure to defy his mother. He knew her sadness and disappointment was real. But the thrill of what he was doing, the knowledge that he belonged with these two people, was real too.

He realized Dray had said something, a single sharp warning whisper.

'Guards!'

Ayl kept his head down as they came rushing down the corridor, coming right for him. Surely they would recognize Keller! He kept walking, unable to breathe now. There was a mad stampede, boots thumping past, angry voices shouting across the hall.

Their adventure was over already. He could feel the

exact spot on his shoulder where the guard's hand would come down. It felt cold.

The noises were going away. The guards had rushed past without noticing them.

A familiar voice was cursing – the one who had read that never-ending list of kings of Cantor. Tyrus. 'That kracking boy has run off again!' he roared. 'If you want to keep your jobs, you'd better find him!'

'He won't have gone far!' barked a Trade Council captain, urging his squad past. One of the guards knocked into Ayl, nearly sending his laundry flying. Ayl saw a smudge of Insta-Tan on the man's arm and braced himself for the shout of discovery. But the guard didn't stop.

Keller nudged them through a set of double doors that swung loosely back and forth. A hot, sickly-rich blast of air hit Ayl in the face, making him feel queasy for a moment. From the shiny metal sinks and the hubbub of activity, he knew they had to be in the kitchens.

'Tablecloths, is it?' somebody shouted to them. Ayl realized they must mean the linen. 'About time!' Get 'em through to the back!'

The place was heaving with people shouting orders, insults and excuses. The coronation might have been postponed, but the guests still needed to be fed. Ayl kept his head resolutely down, staying cool, focusing on walking.

He put on a burst of speed to catch up with the others. Then he stopped. There was blood on the floor, and a stench of death in his nostrils.

He had to glance up. A huge Cantorian was hacking an animal's carcass into chops. A gobbet of flesh flew past his nose.

Ayl frowned before he could stop himself. Nobody on Aquanthis ate other creatures, nor had they done for thousands of turns. Being here in this grisly place was like visiting some nasty earlier chapter in evolution.

The cook caught his eye, and frowned. 'What you sneering at, kid?' Bloodied fingers reached out towards Ayl.

Then everyone looked around as the doors burst open. A squad of Trade Council guards came barrelling into the kitchen. 'Everybody stand where you are!' screeched their commander. 'Nobody move!'

'I see him!' a guard yelled.

Ayl heard Dray mutter, 'So much for stealth!' She grabbed him and Keller by a wrist each and dragged them round the corner to where a huge door made of metal slats was slowly descending. A delivery point, Ayl realized. A goods skimmer was still there on the other side, orange lights flashing, about to pull away.

Together they ducked under the descending door and came up on the other side, a deserted gully between palace buildings. Ayl heard guards yelling and banging, trying to fight their way through. A fist thumped a control. The door halted its descent, then reversed. Ayl saw boots.

'Here!' Dray yelled. The goods skimmer was an auto-piloted shallow truck with an open cage on the back, half-full of crates. Dust flew up from beneath as it hovered on its cushion of invisible force. They vaulted over the safety rail and hunkered down in the back.

The goods skimmer lurched and began to move, slowly at first, then faster.

'Can we steer this thing?' Dray asked.

Keller shook his head. 'They're pre-programmed.'

'So . . . where are we going?' Ayl asked.

'Anywhere but here,' Keller replied, his face grim.

7

Keller crouched low among the crates, hidden from sight. He pressed his body up against the loose crates, hoping it would keep them from smashing around loosely inside the back. The goods skimmer didn't know it had human passengers, and slammed the vehicle round corners like a maniac.

Keller badly wanted to peer over the tops of the crates and see where they were going, but the last time he'd tried that, Dray had pulled him back down with a warning glare.

With nothing else to do, he pondered the markings on the containers. They had contained 'Unprocessed Wasp-Corn', 'Battery Farmed Phlab', 'Assorted Singegrass' and 'Vat-Grown Fungal Cake, 24 Units'. Delightful. The smell in the back of the skimmer was bizarre, like a cross between deep earthy roots, sour milk and incense.

He sat up abruptly. 'We're slowing down.'

The others agreed. The hum of the craft's engines was growing deeper.

'Yeah, but let's wait till we stop,' Ayl warned. 'We can't just jump out of a moving – oh, for krack's sake, Dray!'

She had already vaulted out of the skimmer, landed and rolled in the dirt. Keller jumped after her.

'Good plan,' Keller gasped. 'Might be someone waiting for us at the other end.'

There was a yell. They turned around. Ayl had fallen and was flopping in the dust like a landed fish. With a laugh, Keller went and helped him up.

'Where *are* we?' Ayl said.

'Well . . . we're still on Cantor,' said Keller breezily. 'So don't panic!'

But as he looked around at the ramshackle landscape of slums that surrounded them, he wondered if they had somehow slipped through a wormhole into another, poorer, more desperate world. This was far from the Cantor he knew.

They were in a dusty side road that led up to a street market. The houses crammed together on either side, little more than sheds, were jury-rigged from scrap and salvage. Polythene sheets stapled in place served as windows. Keller glanced into one house as he passed by.

A group of people were cooking a small pot of soup over a chemical burner, which sizzled and stank. Those burners were meant to be used in factories, Keller knew, not for cooking food.

Across the street, a skinny girl was ladling dirty rainwater from a re-used plastic barrel. With a shock, Keller recognized the logo emblazoned on its side. Mazakomi hi-burn fuel, the same he used in his racing ship.

She ran up to him, holding her open hands out for money. 'Pleathe?' she said, and Keller saw her mouth was blistered inside. 'Pleathe help?'

'I'm sorry . . . I haven't any money on me,' he mumbled. It was true, but he felt wretched saying it.

How could he explain to her that he never *needed* to carry money? In the palace, all he had to do was ask for whatever he wanted, and he got it. For everything else, there was his platinum credit slates. Asking this girl if she accepted credit slates would be a sick joke.

He walked on, leaving her standing there. When he turned and looked back at the bottom of the street, she was still staring after him.

There were more beggars as they walked, some adults; many children. A great many of them were injured, sick, or both.

'I had no idea parts of Cantor were like this,' Dray said.

Keller didn't answer. He was thinking the same thing himself. In the sumptuous comfort of the palace he'd never really questioned how the rest of Cantor lived.

Ayl shaded his eyes. 'I think that's the spaceport conning tower!' he said, pointing over the roofs. 'Which means we're not far from the capital.'

'Look at this!' Dray said. 'It's not a bad likeness, is it?' She was pointing up at a poster showing Keller's face in profile, stylized rays emanating from it. The text below gave today's date and the slogan 'Long Live the King' in bold letters.

'That's the great thing about a coronation,' Keller said. 'Really brings the planet together.'

'I'm not sure if everyone would agree,' Ayl said quietly.

He gestured to a wall that had been plastered with hundreds of those same posters. As Keller drew closer, he saw every single one had been scrawled on in angry red paint.

The same words were repeated. DOWN WITH THE TYRANTS. GIVE US BREAD NOT BRATS. SAME LIES DIFFERENT FACE.

Keller stared at a hundred images of himself dripping with words of anger and hate. In some of the posters his eyes had been blacked out, making him look ghoulish. A flesh-eating zombie, preying on the common people. That was how they saw him.

'Keller, come on.' Dray was tugging at his arm. He followed her, one thought burning in his mind. *If this is what my people think of me, no wonder someone tried to blow my brains out.*

Dray was losing patience. 'Ayl, what's wrong? Can't you move any faster?'

'Hey! This isn't my environment, OK? You want to try staying underwater for an hour and see how you like it?'

'Sorry. I guess I forgot.'

'I'll be fine if I can just get out of this sun,' Ayl said. 'Insta-Tan or no, my skin's going to start flaking off if I don't.'

Dray gestured toward a long block-built structure with a sloping metal roof and a small adjoining lobby. 'In here.'

There was shade inside the lobby, but the heat was even worse than outside. This place was stuffy – a factory of some kind. Dray heard the clatter of machinery and the sound of hundreds of tools at work.

86

Curious, she peered through a greenish plastic interior window into the main building.

Hunched over benches that ran the entire length of the hall were rows of miserable creatures. Some were Cantorians dressed in rags, but others were members of species Dray had never seen before. Some were crablike, some like pot-bellied hairless apes, some sucker-fingered carp-lipped things that seemed to be struggling with the gravity.

They were cutting fabric, stitching, sealing seams with heat guns. Others worked at the larger machines against the wall, snatching freshly cut fabric before the blades came down again. Dray saw stained bandages on hands and fingers, and remembered the beggars with their injuries.

At the end of the hall was a Cantorian, his flabby upper body bare. He swigged from a flask and ran a slim leather whip through his fingers. Behind him were stacked piles of clothes. And there was a stack of brocade fabric in long rolls, its glorious textures shining in gold, blue, emerald and scarlet.

'Keller,' Dray said in disgust. 'That's the same fabric your coronation robes are made of. Isn't it?'

Keller's face had turned the colour of curdled milk.

A small, hairy alien fumbled his heat gun and

scorched a black mark down the cloth he was working on. The supervisor noticed instantly. Despite the worker's gibbering plea, the supervisor grabbed him with a beefy hand and dragged him up in front of the others.

Dray bared her teeth.

'Clumsiness costs!' the supervisor shouted above the din. 'You all know the penalty for damaging your cloth. Fifteen lashes!'

The whip unfurled like the sting of some obscene beast, and lashed across the trembling worker's back. His thin scream was lost among the noise of work. Nobody even looked up.

The supervisor drew back his arm for a second blow. Dray kicked the doors open with a noise like a rifle shot. As the workers and the supervisor all gaped at her, she flung her bladed throwing disk.

It hummed through the air, too fast to see, and thunked into the wall. The severed whip fell to the floor, leaving the handle in the supervisor's hand.

He looked at it and back at her. 'Who the hell are *you*?' he bellowed.

'I'm someone who spits on cowards like you,' Dray said, taking another step forward.

'You got some nerve, girl. How I keep my workers in

line is my business.'

'Beating up somone unarmed? You're filth.'

The supervisor raised a fist. 'You want knocking about a bit too? Fine. We'll have some fun. Hope you like tasting blood.'

'Oh, I'm looking forward to tasting *yours*.'

They faced one another, only a few paces apart. Dray studied his ugly face. Even without her visor, she knew exactly where to strike. A blow to the pressure point just behind the jaw would drop this sack of guts like a rock.

Keller stepped between them, holding up a hand. 'Stop! By order of the Trade King of Cantor, there will be no more beatings here!'

Ayl cowered in the doorway, hearing the big man's scornful laughter. 'Is that a fact? You snot-nosed little . . . Zab! Morkus! Get in here and help me beat some manners into these two!'

From a side door, two more burly Cantorians came charging in: one tall, the other short. The workers looked on fearfully, some doing their best to carry on working.

The supervisor came for Dray, swinging his fist like a meaty sledgehammer. She leapt and spun in the air, landing a quick elbow jab on the side of his head. There was a businesslike crack, like someone breaking a pencil. His face took on a vacant, stupid expression, and his legs seemed to give way from under him.

Dray dodged out of the way as the man's huge mass toppled and impacted on the floor. Workers nearby screamed in fear.

Keller ducked into the space between two rows of workbenches, but each of the heavies took an end, and they closed in on him. Trapped, he could only grab a heat gun from the bench and fire spits of scalding sealant at them.

'Ayl! Help!' Keller yelled. One of the heavies, the taller one, grabbed Keller from behind. The short one punched him in the stomach, knocking the wind out of him.

'I can't!' Ayl protested. Fight? He could no more fight than he could fly. Memories of the slaying in his recent past came bubbling up, the moment when he'd taken a life, and he just froze to the spot. What if he killed someone again?

Dray jumped on to the workbench, kicking tools and cloth out of her way. She ran along the tabletop to where the two men had Keller trapped. Dray lashed out at the short one with a kick, but the man was faster and grabbed her by the ankle.

Ayl couldn't believe it. People didn't just out-fight Dray. He took a couple of steps forward, then froze again.

The short Cantorian was half-carrying, half-dragging the kicking, punching Bellori girl and pulling her across the room towards the machines.

'Kill her,' the taller thug yelled, still holding Keller. 'She's dangerous, that one.'

Keller struggled in the man's grip. 'Ayl, *do something*!'

Ayl had no idea what to do. He could only watch, like the audience at an execution, as the man got ready to throw Dray into the cutting machine. The rollers and blades would rip her to shreds in clicks. She fought, biting and tearing at him, but he didn't seem to feel it.

'Don't struggle,' the man grunted. 'It'll be over much quicker if you keep still.'

A sudden flash of pure anger lit up Ayl's mind then, from somewhere deep within, older and more primitive than his Aquanth upbringing. He saw a teetering stack of fabric, close to the stupid, brutal man.

Fall. Crush. Bury him!

And his mind was suddenly lashing out, unseen currents of force pummelling the air. The bolts of fabric leapt free as if a ghostly hand had shoved them. The man glanced up just as the stifling avalanche came down on him. Dray tugged herself free and ran for it.

The other thug, yelling wildly, fought to dig his comrade out. Pandemonium broke out as the workers desperately tried to clear up the mess. A few of the braver ones, seeing their chance for freedom, were climbing out of the windows.

Dray pulled Keller to his feet. 'Let's get out of here! Run!'

Keller slapped Ayl's back as they ran into the street. 'Incredible! What did you *do* back there?'

'I don't know,' Ayl panted. 'I . . . I just don't know!'

8

Dray's blood was up. She could hear the two factory brutes yelling and cursing close behind.

'That's one I owe you!' she yelled to Ayl. 'Full of surprises, aren't you, Blue?'

Ayl smiled sheepishly.

'Which way?' panted Keller.

'Head for the market!' Dray said. 'We'll lose them in the crowds!'

They cut through a back alley. A group of lean, gas-masked figures were playing some sort of game with pieces made from recycled data slates. Black lenses turned to look at Dray as they ran past, and a robed claw came up, maybe to invite them to the game, maybe to snatch at them.

Dray ducked out of the way and kept running. She could see the brightly coloured fabric canopies of the market up ahead, and smelled raw leather and hot food.

They burst into the market between a stall selling

93

crude weaponry made from re-used bits of scrap metal and a food merchant passing out cones of greasy paper, with what looked like lengths of fried tentacle nesting in them.

Dray glanced back over her shoulder. The alleyway was empty, but their two pursuers could come around the corner any moment. They quickly joined the flow of the crowd, dodging between people.

The market wound down a central street, filling it up with multicoloured sections like a parade dragon. Holo-projectors beamed images of exotic produce above some of the stalls, bearing no resemblance to the shoddy goods on offer.

The babble of sound was amazing. Stalls blared music out into the street. A living stream of humans and aliens from various planets wound through and around the stalls, and almost all of them had something to shout about. Two Urkuns, hoods drawn up over their bear-like heads, shared a loud joke. A Cantorian howled in agony, bent over a chair, as a long-armed Slivith etched a laser tattoo into his smoking back.

On all sides, angry buyers haggled over prices. Traders shouted out their wares: hacked com-links, pirated simcasts, clothes, incense, even medicine. Dray recognized a bright pink box of children's antibiotic patches. It was selling at an outrageous price.

She looked back again. Nobody coming. 'I think we're in the clear.'

Keller slowed to a walk, his bruised face contorted with pain and fatigue. 'That's a shame. I was enjoying the exercise.'

They made their way through the crowds, jostled and bumped by heedless passers-by. Dray tried to avoid catching anyone's eye, in case they took it as an invitation to a fight. They had to keep moving and not draw attention.

Before long, Dray's gaze was drawn to yet another weapons stall. 'Combat knife!' the trader gushed, noticing her before she could move away. He was a Cyclopic: squat and froglike. 'Bellori manufacture. Best in system. Help protect you, little lady.'

He held up a blade Dray recognized as a kitchen cutter. The moulded polymer handle was trying to look like it came from a Bellori *scratha* knife. And failing.

'You like?' the trader grinned toothlessly, blinking his one eye. 'For you, fifteen.'

Keller tapped her on the shoulder. 'Ask him about the bullet,' he whispered. 'He's a weapons seller, isn't he? Maybe he knows something.'

'Why don't *you* ask him?' Dray hissed back. 'I ought

to put his lights out! Trying to pass off that piece of krack as a Bellori blade!'

'I can't. He might recognize me.'

'I wouldn't count on it,' Dray said drily, looking Keller up and down. With his black eye, tousled hair and dishevelled clothing, the trade king didn't look much like the image on the coronation posters. 'But if you're worried, I'll ask.'

Dray knew there was no way the trader would suspect she was Bellori without her armour. She brandished the crushed bullet at the trader. 'Look at this. Tell me everything you know about it.'

The trader's broad mouth scowled. 'I no like you manners very much, girl.'

'Start talking, or you'll regret it.'

The trader leaned threateningly over his stall. Dray noticed he was wearing stun-nux on his fist. 'I think you better start *walking*. Or *you* regret it.'

Keller was already pulling her away. With a last glare over her shoulder, she went with him.

'Well, that was productive,' Ayl observed.

'Try asking that guy with the sunglasses over there, the one selling all those off-world gizmos,' Keller suggested. 'And this time, try not to be so . . .'

'Bellori?' said Dray frostily.

'Yeah. That.'

The grinning, suntanned hawker peered over his sunglasses as they approached, and Dray caught a momentary glimpse of glowing cybernetic eyes. 'And what can I offer you, young people?' he asked breezily.

'What do you know about bullets like this?' Dray said, holding it up.

The grin didn't falter. 'Well, missy, that depends on who's asking, dunnit?'

'I'm someone who needs to know. That's all I'm telling you.'

The hawker folded his arms. 'Word of advice. People round here don't like too many questions bein' asked. It's bad for business.' He leaned close and hissed, 'Push off while you've still got the legs to carry you.'

Keller was already storming away. 'This is pointless!'

'What did you expect from me, Keller?' Dray scowled. 'Curtsies and simpering? I told you I didn't want to do it.'

'Oh, it doesn't matter. We can't ask every trader if they know anything; there's just too many of them. Unless . . .' A gleam came into Keller's eye as he looked at Ayl.

'Unless what?'

'Unless Ayl can read their minds.'

* * *

Ayl didn't register Keller's suggestion at first. Since the factory, he'd been absorbed in his own thoughts, the world around him moving past like a dream.

He knew he'd moved the fabric with his mind. It wasn't a coincidence; he'd felt the mental force shoving against the heavy rolls. What he couldn't understand was how he'd done it.

It was like some new ability had awoken in him, bursting out of the cells of his body. But did that mean all Aquanths had latent telekinetic abilities? Or was he actually a freak of nature, some random mutation branching off from the evolutionary tree?

His mother might know. He reached out to her with his mind – then stopped. No, he couldn't lean on her any more. This was his new current to swim in, and he'd do it alone.

The thought that he might be abnormal both terrified and comforted him. If he was genuinely different, that meant he was right to feel like an outsider among his own people. It wasn't his fault that he didn't fit in.

But to be the only one of your kind, hailing from a planet where unity was all-important . . . it was the ultimate nightmare!

Dray's finger prodded him in the side. 'Hey, wake up, Blue!'

'Huh . . . what?' he said. 'Sorry, guys. I was thinking.'

Keller repeated his request.

'Read their minds? Yeah, that should be possible,' Ayl glanced around him. 'It's kind of uncivilized, though. Poking about where you've not been invited, you know?'

'We don't have a choice!' Keller insisted.

Ayl closed his eyes. He expanded the field of his mind, gently swelling it outward like an invisible soap bubble.

Other people's thoughts immediately swam into his consciousness, a wild chitter-chatter of overheard conversations and internal mutterings. The merchants' minds were babbling busily: *Ten for that, you must be mad . . . there's another one caught and done for and no tax to pay!* Some minds were full of alien gibberish: *CH'KA MO TAKRUB LO HARA! BRESNI! BRESNI!* And there were the thoughts of a would-be thief, no louder than a whisper: *Easy does it, they'll never notice. Whatever you do, don't look at your hands when you're stealing.*

'Getting anything?' Keller asked.

Ayl held up a warning hand. He needed Keller not

99

to interrupt. Ayl concentrated, threw open the doors of his mind and overheard someone praying: *Please, powers of mercy, let me be safe now . . . let the giant spiders not find me here . . .*

Ayl focused on that last one. A small, frightened alien, huddled in a disused archway. He was thinking of his homeworld. Orgren, that was its name.

Safe here on Cantor, yes, safe among all the people. The giant spiders will not come here to ravage and destroy like they did on Orgren . . .

Ayl saw the image of a 'giant spider' in the alien's memory. He had already known what it would be.

'Nara-Karith!' he muttered under his breath. Hadn't he known, all along, that they were back?

More confident now, he widened the scan. Random Cantorian thoughts came flooding into his mind, mostly from the beggars this time. *Welcome to another kracking day in paradise . . . I'm starving . . . Someone took a shot at the Keller boy, shame they missed . . . Slave all your life and what do you get.*

All so miserable, all so alike. Nothing of any use. He moved from mind to mind, amazed at how easy it was becoming. He sifted through thoughts as if he were panning for gold, hunting for the gleam of information.

There! Only two words, but they were enough. *Purple robe.*

Ayl zoomed in on the thought's owner: one of the traders, tucked away in a backstreet. A greasy, leather-clad Cantorian, selling stolen data slates from the back of a hoverbike. He caught a bit of gabble about a 'stranger'. Then, before he could see any more, the trader began thinking about a warehouse he was going to break into later on.

He snapped back to reality, and told the others what he'd seen.

'He's thinking about something else now,' said Ayl. 'We'll have to talk to him.'

'This time,' Keller said as Ayl led them through to the twisting back street, 'let *me* do the talking!'

When they found the man, he gave a guilty start. 'What you want to go sneaking up on me like that for?'

'Didn't mean to startle you,' Keller said. 'Just wanted to chat, if that's all right.'

'Yeah, well, as it happens, I'm closing up for the afternoon,' said the trader, hastily beginning to pack the data slates away.

'We'll make it worth your while,' said Keller, smiling. 'Five hundred ought to do it. I take it you accept platinum credit slates?'

The trader's eyes widened as he took the slate and jammed it into a reader. 'Where did you . . . never mind. Go on, then. What do you need to know?'

Dray showed him the bullet.

He looked suddenly uncomfortable. 'I've seen this before,' he admitted. 'Took some bullets just like it as payment, along with this weird gun. Had a sort of spider crest on it. Bloke said he didn't want to deal in cash, so I took the gun and bullets.'

'Payment for what?' Keller asked.

'Nothing illegal! Just a robe, all right? A purple robe!' Pale and thin-lipped now, the trader began to fling his wares into the back of his bike. 'You've had your money's worth. Get lost.'

'The person who wanted the robe – what did he look like?'

The man just shook his head and remained silent.

Keller and Dray exchanged glances.

Dray grabbed the startled trader by the lapels. Before he could resist, she flung him to the ground, wrapped one arm around his neck and held him in a headlock. Data slates went scattering across the alley cobbles.

'Can't . . . breathe!' the trader gurgled.

'Answer the question and you can have all the air

you want,' Keller said. 'I won't even charge you for it. Tell me what the person you sold the robe to looked like!'

'Big!' spluttered the trader. 'Pushy – threatened to rip my spine out. Deep voice. Had this alien with him, big one, never seen it before . . .'

Dray let the man breathe. 'What did *that* look like?' she demanded.

'Like a spider!' the man snivelled. 'A giant spider!'

'Let him go, Dray,' Keller told her.

As the man scrambled away, coughing and rubbing his neck, the three friends shared anxious glances. Keller knew they were both thinking the same as him.

Their worst fears were confirmed. The Nara-Karith were back.

'It doesn't make sense,' Keller said, as they walked back towards the market. 'We destroyed them. My father died fighting them. How can they be back?'

'Let's worry about that later,' said Dray. 'I'm starving. I haven't eaten since I left Bellus.'

Keller realized all this had happened in less than a single cycle. It seemed insane.

'That place looks as good as any,' he said, pointing to a grimy food stall. People sat at long benches, glumly picking morsels out of polycard trays. It reminded Keller of the factory.

'You guys sit down,' he said. 'I'll buy.' He joined the queue, looking at his feet and hoping he wouldn't be recognized.

Moments later they were staring down at trays of their own, where lumps of unidentifiable matter swam in yellow grease. Keller tried a bite. It tasted like mildew and sweat, with a faint aftertaste of burned flesh.

'I was looking forward to the coronation feast all morning,' he muttered. 'Can't say I was expecting this muck.'

'I'm not sure I can eat this,' Ayl said, fishing a tangle of matted hair out of his tray. 'I'm a vegetarian.'

'Don't worry,' Dray said. 'I'm pretty sure this isn't real meat. Or real vegetables.'

Two men in long overcoats sat down beside the group. 'Shove up, lad,' one of them said to Keller.

'What about that shooter at the palace, then?' said the other man, through a mouthful of mush. 'Nearly snuffed the new king right there on the spot.'

'What a pity,' his friend said with heavy sarcasm. 'I've had a gutful of these trade kings. They get richer and richer, while we get poorer.'

The other nodded. 'If the fella that shot him was here, I'd shake his hand. Little brat had it coming.'

Keller cringed in his seat. *If my own people don't want me as their king, why should I put up with the hassle?* he thought. I'm done. *Tyrus can choke on his beard for all I care.*

They ate in silence until the men had gone. Then Ayl whispered, 'I knew the Nara-Karith were behind this. I've known since before it happened. I sensed it.'

'It just isn't possible!' Dray said, thumping the table. 'The Nara-Karith couldn't have escaped the asteroid! And whoever shot Keller was humanoid. The trader said so.'

'They're back, Dray,' said Ayl. 'We all know it. Let's not lie to ourselves. Not when we're the only ones on this whole planet who know the truth.'

'He's right,' Keller said simply. Nightmares were rising back out of the darkness of the recent past. He wished more than ever that he could simply turn the clock back and have his father alive again.

'Hey! That's them!'

Trade Council guards were moving through the crowd towards them, shoving pedestrians out of the way.

Keller swung his legs over the bench and sprinted for dear life, hoping the others were following. He knocked over a table, sending food and hot drinks flying. Angry yells rang in his ears. From behind came another crash as Dray threw a table over, forming a makeshift barricade.

The guards were back on their tail, only a few paces behind, and he had no idea where to run.

9

Dray thought, *These goons would be no threat if I still had my armour.*

But as she sprinted through the market, without the weight of her armour, she was as fast and agile as a wildcat.

'Follow me!' she yelled back to the others.

She raced through the market, running between and around the oncoming tide of pedestrians. Duck, weave, vault and leap – it was like the training course back on Bellus, running against an oncoming wall of infantry. She slipped easily back into her military mindset.

The Trade Council guards yelled angrily from somewhere behind her. Any moment now, a shot could ring through the air. She zigzagged wildly, making herself as hard a target as she could. The guards probably wouldn't use lethal force against them – but then again, Keller was the only one whose life they cared about.

A quick glance over her shoulder told Dray that Ayl and Keller were right behind. Suddenly, from a side alley, a wiry Grunmuk trader pedalled a fruit-laden trike out into the road. It was directly in her path.

Dray put on a burst of speed and sprang, soaring clear over the fruit trolley and landing heavily on the other side. A street musician whooped in appreciation and began to applaud.

From behind came a tremendous crash as a produce stall went over. Dray span around to see Keller running away from a spilled, spreading heap of purple shadowtubers and tumbling yellow phosphruit.

The falling stall yanked a suspended line from its moorings. Dangling bags of spices fell and exploded like grenades, sending up clouds of thick smoky dust.

'What you think you doing?' screeched a trader from somewhere inside the cloud. 'You know how much this is *worth*? Come back! Idiot boy!'

'Sorry!' Keller shouted across the wreckage. 'I'll pay for it, I promise!'

'Where's Blue?' Dray said. The spices in the air were burning her throat, making her cough. 'Did they get him?'

Keller pointed to where Ayl was scrambling out of the spice cloud. The Aquanth had turned the burnt orange colour of curried kreshbeast.

Keller shrugged. 'He's changed colour again, but he looks OK!'

'Make for the market square!' Dray yelled. She set off at a run. She'd just have to hope the destroyed stall slowed the Trade Council guards down. From the infuriated shouts and crashing, splintering sounds, they were causing some property damage of their own as they tried to fight their way through. Good.

Behind her, she could hear Keller and Ayl doing their best to keep up, coughing and gasping as they ran. The spice was like tear gas.

Dray rounded the pillared corner of the market hall. The market square opened before her to her right, bustling with Cantorians, aliens and animals, the ugly dome of the traders' hall looming over it all like a scowling ogre's head. Dozens of shadowy alleyways, half-hidden by hanging fabric and close-packed stalls, led off in all directions.

Perfect. One last sprint, and the soldiers would never catch them.

She turned to yell at the others to catch up, just in time to hear Ayl let out a strange wavering cry of pain. He had fallen, his ankle badly twisted.

'Oh, *krack*!' Dray spat. 'That's all we need!'

'Tell me you can still run,' said Keller, ashen-faced.

Ayl limped forward a couple of paces and fell.

'Run, you two,' he said, clutching his ankle. 'Get out of here! Don't worry about me – just go!'

Dray and Keller gave each other a look. Without a word, they both reached down and grabbed one of Ayl's arms. Between them, they hoisted Ayl up and, with his arms around their necks, they ran. Dray silently cursed – the guards would be bound to see them now.

'Head for the market hall!' she said through gritted teeth. It was spilling over with people, more than enough to hide them.

They shoved through the crowds, ignoring the mutters and raised voices, and pressed up against the inside wall. From outside, Dray heard shouting.

'They'll have headed down one of those alleys! Split up and search for them!'

The Trade Council guards went pounding past outside. Dray waited until the tramping feet had died away completely, then allowed herself a huge sigh of relief.

I'm covered in spice dust, Keller thought. *I'm wearing a servant's uniform, and my face is bruised from those mullocks at the sweatshop. I don't look much like a trade king. Maybe I can relax now, just for a minute.*

Someone tapped him on the shoulder and he jumped. He turned around, certain he'd been recognized.

'Here,' said a bored-sounding attendant, passing a data slate to him and two more to Ayl and Dray. 'You're late. Auction's already been running half an hour.' Jerking her head in the direction of the main hall, she moved on through the crowd, handing out more data slates.

Moving with the flow of the crowd, the three of them headed further through the entrance hall, opening up the data slates as they went and pretending to read the contents.

Keller felt a little better. He could hide his face behind this thing and nobody would think it strange.

The slate was obviously a guide to the auction that was going on, but Keller couldn't figure out what was being sold. Livestock, probably, or perhaps farm equipment. *Lot 5 – One Carboxian: very robust, good breeding potential. Lot 6 – Three Maltramics: previously owned, sold as seen.*

They filed into the main hall and shuffled along the wall at the back, trying not to draw attention to themselves. At the front was a podium, empty except for a folded black device that resembled a metal shrub.

An auctioneer in a pressed suit peered impatiently out over the crowd.

'No Trade Council guards in here, at least,' whispered Dray.

'Can't say I feel much safer,' Keller replied. The crowd in here was an intimidating collection of huge men in long coats with dark eye-visors, hollow-cheeked women tapping manicured nails on their slates, scowling mercenary types and fat merchants. As Keller moved to a spot with a good view, he drew many sullen glares and threatening mutters.

A tall man with a cadaverous face leaned across and whispered in his ear, making him shudder: 'You'll be bidding on the Vespic female, I expect?'

'I'm keeping my options open,' Keller said casually.

'Don't waste your money,' the man said, laying his hand on Keller's shoulder. 'She's infested with psychomites. Cost a fortune to delouse.'

'Thanks,' Keller said, moving away from the man's grasp. His skin was crawling all over like *he* had psychomites.

A horrible suspicion was beginning to form in his mind. The auction wasn't for farm equipment. It wasn't for livestock, either – although people like this would probably say that it was.

When they dragged the whimpering stoop-shouldered alien out and hauled it up to the podium, Keller knew his suspicions were right. The alien was being pulled by a chain around his scrawny neck. When he reached the podium, the device unfolded itself and wound long robotic tentacles around his ankles, locking him in place.

This was a slave auction.

'Now,' the auctioneer said. 'Lot 7 – One Threp. As you can see, the aggression glands have been surgically removed, making the creature docile and spineless. Who will open the bidding at fifty credits? Do I hear fifty?'

Two rows in front of Keller, a flabby man held up his data slate. Keller's heart suddenly lurched. It was the overseer from the sweatshop, with his two bruisers on either side of him. He seemed none the worse from having been knocked out by Dray earlier on.

If he turned around, he'd see Keller – and the hall was packed with people now, with no easy way out.

'Thank you, sir. Any advance on fifty?'

Another data slate appeared above the crowd, upping the bid. The overseer immediately raised his again.

Keller felt like the eyes of the world were suddenly focused on him, a stare penetrating him to the soul.

This was his planet. He was meant to be its king. And here, in front of him, was stark proof that Cantor not only tolerated slavery, it profited from it.

He flashed back to the image of his coronation robes. Such rich, sumptuous Tevekarian brocade. What a deal he'd struck. And now, the hapless alien in front of him was being sold for a fraction of the price he'd paid. Sold to a man who would put him to work weaving the same material. The machine would keep turning, and Cantor's merchants would keep pocketing the profits of slavery.

'Sold, to the gentleman at the back, for eighty standard credits. Next up, Lot 8 – a Belphegorian male, in prime condition, with all its heads intact and certified.'

Keller watched in horror as a three-headed creature with a muscular body was led to the podium. Had his father known about this? Surely he must have done, but how could he have let it go on?

I knew we were traders, he thought. *But I never knew we traded in lives. They say a Cantorian will buy and sell anything. It looks like they were right.*

'Starting the bidding at three hundred. Do I hear three hundred?'

Keller twisted the ring on his finger. *I'm in charge*

now, he thought. *And I'm not letting this go on any longer.*

'What are you doing?' Dray said in a warning whisper.

'I'm putting a stop to this,' Keller said. 'I've got the authority.'

'You can't!'

'Watch me.'

'Keller, it makes me sick too, but we can't attract attention to ourselves!'

Keller pointed his data slate at the Belphegorian. 'You want to tell him that?' he hissed. '"Sorry, you don't get to go free today, we were too scared for our own skins?"'

'You idiot, someone will see . . .' Dray grabbed at Keller's arm, trying to pull it down out of sight. The data slate waved in the air as he struggled with her.

'Five hundred from the young man at the back!' called the auctioneer, nodding at Keller's data slate. 'Any advance on five hundred?'

Murmuring broke out. 'New bidder?' 'Not one of ours . . .' 'Good choice, m'lad.' 'What's he know that we don't?'

Every face in the hall turned to look at him. The cadaverous man standing alongside had a puzzled expression, as if he was trying to work out where he'd seen Keller before. Beside him, Dray tensed, ready for a fight.

Now I've got their attention, I should seize the moment.

'I'm not bidding,' he said, his voice ringing loud and clear across the room. 'I'm closing this auction down right now!'

'On whose authority?' demanded the auctioneer.

'On my own!'

The sweatshop overseer's eyes bulged in his head as he recognized Keller.

'I know that voice!' he sneered. 'Tried to close my business down earlier, didn't you? Well, you won't get away this time!'

A voice from somewhere in the crowd shouted, 'Hey, that's the new trade king!'

Keller caught the flash of Trade Council guards' helmets moving through the crowd. The overseer and his right-hand-man were shoving people aside, trying to reach him.

'Dray,' Keller said quickly, 'grab Blue and follow me. We're getting out of here!'

He charged through the crowd, heading for the main exit, praying he wasn't running headlong into a trap. Though with the guards and the goons from the sweatshop both on his tail, things could hardly get any worse.

'Are you mad?' he heard someone yell to the overseer. 'That's King Lial's son!'

'I don't care who he is!' the overseer bellowed. 'When I get my hands on him, he's dead meat!'

'Blue! Climb on, quick!'

Ayl threw his arms around Dray's neck and clung on. She hoisted him as if she were helping a wounded soldier off the battlefield, and ran through the shouting, jeering crowd towards Keller's retreating back. Her run jolted his ankle, making it throb.

Despite his pain and fear, he felt awe. Dray wasn't flagging at all. The muscles in her arms and back felt like knots of steel cable.

They burst out of the market hall, down the steps and out into the open air. Ayl could sense their pursuers' hostility, like a wave gathering strength behind them. Fragments of their angry thoughts echoed in his mind.

'Which way?' Keller called back desperately.

'Pick an alley!' Dray yelled. 'Just do it fast!'

Keller ducked down an alleyway next to a Velanish fortune-teller, who was rattling her cupful of bones for a worried-looking client. Ayl held on tight as Dray followed after. The fortune-teller shook her head as they passed and clicked her tongue.

Ayl glanced behind him. The alley had high, sheer walls. If they were cornered here, there would be no way to escape.

Up ahead, he heard Keller groan, 'Oh, *krack*!'

To Ayl's dismay, the alley ended in a blank wall. Heaps of garbage lay nestled in the corners. There was a half-hidden door through to the other side, reinforced with strips of plasteel.

Dray set Ayl down while Keller rattled the handle uselessly. 'No good. It's locked!'

'Dray? Can you break through?'

'Not in the time we've got,' Dray said sadly. She turned on her heel and began to walk back down the alley.

Ayl stared after her. Their pursuers would be on them any moment, and she was walking right into their hands!

'Dray, wait!'

She kept walking.

'Dray!' he pleaded. 'You can't just give up!'

Dray walked on for a few paces before turning around. She concentrated for a moment, then ran full tilt down the alley. At the last moment she leapt, caught the top of the wall with both hands and hung. She pulled herself up, scrabbling with her feet, and finally sat astride the wall, panting hard.

She held a hand down. Ayl grabbed her arm and held on as she lifted him up. His feet dangled and his ankle struck the wall in an instant of blinding agony. One quick move, and he was straddling the wall next to her.

Keller looked up at them both, his face twisted in sheer panic. 'They're coming!'

'Ready, Blue?' Dray said, sweat beading her face.

Ayl nodded. They reached down and took one of Keller's arms each. They heaved.

'Oh, spirits of Aquanthis, this is not going to be easy!' gasped Ayl. Keller was heavy, his arms and hands slippery with sweat. It was like hauling a young whale out of the sea. Ayl gripped the wall with his legs, the pain in his ankle like a bursting balloon.

Dray let out a long, rising yell, they pulled together, and suddenly Keller was sprawling on top of the wall, gasping up at the sky.

'Get them!' shrieked a voice from the shadows at the alley's end. Staccato bursts of gunfire echoed down the high walls.

'Down!' Dray yelled, flinging herself off the wall. Keller jumped down and Ayl followed, knowing it was going to hurt. He landed feet first, and pain shot through his ankle.

'It's a transport dock,' Dray said. The wind from something large passing by overhead ruffled her hair. The area ahead opened out into a broad, rough circle, marked into zones with lines of bright yellow paint. Hover-lifters, cargo shuttles and short range planet-hoppers were taking off and landing, with dockers busily unloading crates of produce.

'Yeah. For the markets,' said Keller. 'Hey, if we can get on board a transport . . .'

Ayl didn't hear him. He clutched his head. His mind was echoing with alien voices. *Search*, hissed one. *Gather*, rasped another.

'Let's move!' Dray said. 'They'll be over that wall any moment. Blue, come on!'

Ayl shook the voices out of his head, and limped after her.

'Look!' Keller said, pointing to an empty zone. 'Bay 8 is clear. We can run straight across to those hangars on the far side!'

Ayl clung on to Dray's back again. They ran out of the alley, making for the wide open space of Bay 8. As they crossed over the line, there was a deafening howl of engines from directly overhead and a blast of hot, fuel-smelling air.

Ayl looked up to see the filthy metal underside of a cargo transport lowering itself down on them like a collapsing ceiling. He screamed a warning, and Keller and Dray dived out of the way just as the landing struts came down. Orange lights flashed and klaxons blared.

'That was too close,' Keller panted. 'Guess I should have known no bay stays empty for long around here.'

Search! went the voice in Ayl's head, closer and more urgent now. *Gather!*

'I don't want to worry you guys,' he said, 'but I'm pretty sure I can hear the Nara-Karith! Telepathically, I mean. They're somewhere close by.'

Dray pointed. 'Not as close as them!'

The Trade Council guards had found them, and were running across the transport docks. They were carrying stun-dart rifles, just the thing to recapture the fleeing prince.

Ayl glanced back down the alley. The thugs from the sweatshop had reached the top of the wall and were lowering themselves down the other side. The guns they carried looked far more lethal.

'They've got us cornered!' he said.

'Over here!' Keller said triumphantly. He ran to a

hover-bike which had been left with its engine still purring.

Ayl looked around for the driver and saw a man in overalls talking to a warehouse official, a package under his arm. 'Stealing isn't cool,' he muttered, 'but I'm not mad keen on dying, either.'

Dray climbed on behind, with Ayl still clinging to her. The sweatshop heavies saw what was happening, fell to their knees and opened fire on the hover-bike. Amid the shouts from the guards, the yells of dock-workers and the curses of the heavies, they pulled away from the docks and into a stream of oncoming traffic.

Keller leaned over the handlebars and turned the accelerator to max. 'Hold on tight!' he shouted.

10

The hover-bike had been designed for speed, not style. It looked like a slim metal girder with a long foam cushion seat and carrying pods bolted on to the back. On the underside, three metal shapes like radar dishes pointed down at the ground – the anti-grav thrusters. Keller hunched over the handlebars at the front, while Dray held on to the passenger grips behind him and Ayl clung to her waist, sitting on the cargo pods.

Wind roared in Dray's ears. The ground raced by only a few feet below. Keller was pushing the screaming engine way past its safety limits.

'Got to put some distance between us and them!' he shouted above the wind.

A horn blared. A broad-fronted cargo skimmer loomed up in front of them, going too fast to stop.

Dray felt Ayl's grip tighten on her waist. Keller leaned the bike back and they shot right over the oncoming skimmer.

'Keller!' Dray screamed.

Instead of answering, Keller crouched down even further and banked the bike into a wide turn. The road vanished from sight, replaced by patchwork fields and hedgerows that sped past like fast-forwarded vids.

Steadily they angled upwards, pulling away from the ground. The shrubs and bushes were a green blur, the fences a volley of white lines. They were above the treetops now, and climbing.

'Is this thing supposed to fly?' Dray yelled. 'I thought it was a hover-bike!'

'We *are* hovering!' Keller yelled back with a grin. 'We're just hovering very high off the ground!'

They dipped suddenly, coming dangerously close to the topmost branches of an apple orchard. Keller swore, twisted a control, and the bike lurched upward again.

Dray punched Keller in the shoulder. 'Pull over and let me drive!'

'Not a hope!'

'This isn't one of your bloody races! You'll get us all killed!'

Keller laughed. 'You scared?'

'No!' Dray raged. 'I want to die in battle, not plastered over the kracking Cantorian countryside by some hyped-up boy racer!'

'Oh, shut up and enjoy the ride.' Keller waved a hand. 'All this to look at and you're still whining?'

Dray looked out over the land. She didn't want to admit it, but the countryside here on Cantor was beautiful. Fields of crops lay open to the sun, shimmering green and gold, and the patches of woodland were the colour of dark moss on an ancient fortress wall.

Something – the *lack* of something – caught her attention. 'Where are all the rivers?'

'There aren't any,' Keller said. 'All this is reclaimed land. Most of the planet was desert, back in the day.'

She was amazed. 'Cantor was a desert? You mean you *terraformed* all this?'

'Yep! Shipped mega-tanks of water in from Aquanthis on a thousand-turn deal, and put it to use making deserts into fertile land.' He grinned. 'Looks good, doesn't it?'

Dray had to admit it did. Even the high-tech wind turbines and farm buildings looked elegant, graceful white shapes standing out against the sky. From up here it looked like a land of legends, somewhere for warrior heroes to live, not the breadbasket of a pack of greedy merchants.

That was the truth of it, Dray thought. Cantor only

looked like a paradise from up above. She'd seen its true face back in the slums, close up and ugly.

'Yeah, nice planet you've got here, King Keller,' she said acidly. 'Slavery, beatings, hunger, poverty . . . Cantor's got it all.'

'Hey!' yelled Keller, suddenly deadly serious. 'I knew nothing about any of that, OK? As soon as all this has blown over, I'm going to change things!' He gunned the throttle angrily. 'I tried to already, didn't I?'

'I just don't understand how this planet works!' Ayl commented sadly. 'On Aquanthis, everyone's equal. Nobody's better than anyone else.'

'Is that a fact,' said Keller.

'Of course!' Ayl said proudly. 'Everyone is valued!'

'Happy little Aquanths, every single one the same,' said Keller. There was a dangerous edge to his voice that Dray hadn't heard before.

'If everyone gets an equal share without even trying, then why call it *value* at all?' she scoffed. 'We don't give handouts. On Bellus, you have to *earn* respect.'

'Yeah, yeah. By fighting,' Keller said. 'What a surprise.'

Dray wasn't rising to that. 'When you've proved your worth, then you get valued. Not before.'

'So why the krack are you two still here if it's so great

back home?' Keller shot back. 'Why aren't you off on Aquanthis, enjoying all that wonderful equality? And why aren't you back on Bellus, being respected for all the brave things you've done? Hmm?'

Dray didn't have an answer for that.

'Keller?' Ayl shouted. 'Can we stop for a moment?'

'Why? We're not even going that fast any more!' Keller snapped. It was true. The bike had been making erratic wheezing noises for a while.

'It's not that!' Ayl gestured down at a white-walled rectangular structure at the junction of three fields. 'There's water down there. I can heal my ankle with it!'

'That irrigation tank? I guess so.' Keller brought the hover-bike in on a low approach. 'It's not like anyone's following us any more.' His wrist device beeped, signalling an incoming com. He ignored it.

Ayl's palms ached with anticipation. Rather than wait for Keller to park the bike, he waited until they were a few feet over the water's surface, let go of Dray and threw himself off the bike in a backward somersault.

He went under. The water's sudden kiss was magical, rapturous. He swam to the cold concrete bottom of the irrigation tank and lay there in silent ecstasy, wishing every blessing in the world upon whichever Cantorian farmer owned it. This water might have been here on Cantor for many generations or only a few cycles, but either way it had come from Aquanthis originally.

Keller had said so, but Ayl would have known anyway. It tasted of home.

Well-being flooded back into his body. His gills softened and opened. He could feel the torn tissues around his ankle joint begin to knit themselves back together. It was like a rebirth.

He burst out of the water several minutes later, showering the dusty tiles around the tank. Fortunately, nobody was standing nearby.

Dray had a panel open on the back of the hover-bike and was tinkering around inside. Keller was sitting propped up against a wall, squinting up at the sky.

'Thanks, guys,' Ayl said, surfacing and leaning over the side of the tank. 'I needed that.'

'I wish I had my armour,' Dray grumbled. 'There's a complete tool set built into it. I could have this thing patched up and back on the road in five minutes.'

Keller's wrist device beeped again. He took it off and casually threw it over his shoulder, where it landed in a bush. 'Hey, Blue, you're blue again!'

Ayl grinned. He leaned back into the water and

128

began a lazy backstroke to the other side. As he relaxed he let his mind open, wanting to feel the nature of Cantor all around.

Suddenly, his mind was flooded with pain. He saw blood, slashing claws, fire and horror. Screams rang in his ears. His face contorted in agony. As the others rushed over to see what was wrong, he clutched his head and let out a high, thin shriek.

Images of the Nara-Karith were surging through his mind. They were hacking and slashing through a field of purple fruit, and every snap of their pincers seemed to sever a nerve in Ayl's brain. They swarmed, like an insect plague, their scrabbling filling his ears and their limbs scratching painful rents in his consciousness. *Gather*, their voices hissed. *Destroy*.

'Nara-Karith . . . in my head!' he groaned. 'I see them . . .'

Unable to stop the images, he rocked back and forth in the water, trying to take some comfort from it. This was no vision of things to come, he realized. This was happening *now*. The destruction was real.

Eventually, like a storm passing, the horror retreated from his mind. He shook himself and climbed slowly from the tank.

'Are you OK?' Dray asked, helping him out.

'Fine!' he said, wincing and grabbing his head again.

Dray gave him a searching look.

'OK, no,' he admitted. 'Not really. It was a lot stronger that time. Closer.'

He told them what he'd seen: trees ripe with purple fruit, with a swarm of Nara-Karith ravaging the crops.

'That sounds like a samthorn crop.' Keller frowned in thought. 'What else did you see? Buildings, structures, signs, anything like that?'

Ayl thought back. 'No, there wasn't anything – wait. Yes, there was. Some sort of windmill, or wind turbine on a long pole. I saw it above the trees.'

'How many blades?'

'Three. And the pole was twisted, like a spiral.'

'That's a Kastria-Belvine power generator!' Keller said excitedly. 'I know where that is! It's north of here, the Seskavian Valley. They grow samthorn fruit and ship it all over the planet. And the wine they make – it has one of those generators on the label.'

'The bike should stand the trip,' Dray said, 'So long as you don't drive it like a boy racer, of course.'

Soon after, they were heading north past undulating green hills on one side and open plains on the other. The sunset was glorious, but Ayl couldn't see the beauty. His eyes were screwed tight shut. The voices in his head were growing louder, pounding through his brain like pulses of venom.

Gather. Destroy. Gather. Destroy.

'Whoa. This isn't right. This is not right at all.'

Keller checked the nav-bearings on the hover-bike's console. They seemed to be reading correctly. This should be the valley.

But if that was so, then where were the fields of samthorn fruit, ripe for harvest? On either side, there was nothing but flat, stripped land, with smoke still issuing from the scorched stumps of trees.

'Are we in the right place?' Dray asked.

'I think so,' Keller said. 'I mean, I headed the right way . . .'

He brought the bike in to land. Stunned, they walked through the devastation. As soon as he got up close to one of the burned stumps, he knew the truth.

'This is a samthorn tree,' he said. 'Or was. And look.' He pointed up to where a white wind turbine was slowly rotating. 'You saw this happen, didn't you, Ayl?'

The Aquanth didn't answer. He was walking over to three humped, immobile shapes that lay among the ashes.

Gently, he rolled one of them over. A Cantorian's

face stared sightlessly up at them. Ayl turned away and began to retch. Keller didn't even think about mocking him for it.

'They didn't just kill the crops, then,' Dray said quietly. 'Keller—'

'Look at this,' Keller said. 'They fought. They tried to defend the crop.' He was looking down at a long splatter of yellow blood. 'Only Nara-Karith bleed like that.'

'I knew it,' Ayl said, and retched again. 'They're back.'

Keller knelt down. He took a handful of ash and slowly let it trickle through his fingers.

He looked up at Dray, who was watching him with sorrow and respect.

'Shooting at me is one thing,' he said, anger making his voice crack. 'But this? This is an invasion. This is war.'

Dray nodded slowly.

'I want you to witness something for me, Dray,' he said. 'I may not be trade king yet. I may never be. But I swear before all my ancestors and by everything Cantor holds sacred, *I will fight with every drop of blood in my body to protect this planet and the Trinity System!* Do you hear that?'

'I hear you,' said Dray. Her eyes were very bright.

Ayl rejoined them, pale and unsteady still. 'There's a farm building over there,' he said. 'I didn't see it before, because of the trees, but now . . .' He coughed. 'We should check it anyway. Just in case anyone managed to hide.'

Keller didn't want to hope for survivors. It seemed too likely he would be disappointed. But he knew Ayl's words were meant kindly, so he said nothing.

The farm station was a flat-roofed building with tinted glass windows, all but a few of them smashed. Deep gouges had been clawed into the wooden panelling and the front porch was smashed away.

There was a great deal of yellowish blood sprayed across the forecourt. Keller looked from the smoking debris that had once been a transporter to the empty ruin of the farm station, and shook his head. *Nobody could have survived this*, thought Keller. That was how the Nara-Karith operated. Total devastation.

Dray was tugging his arm. 'Keller! Look!'

A face was peeping out from an upper window. Keller saw long, straggly hair and wildly staring eyes.

'It's OK!' he yelled. 'We're friends! We're here to help! We—'

She was gone.

Keller's heart sank – until he saw the front door open, and the woman standing there, trembling.

He approached her, cautiously.

'What happened here?' he asked. 'Who attacked you?'

The woman shook her head. A tiny whimpering sound escaped her lips.

'She's traumatized,' Ayl said. 'I don't think she can speak at all. She's in shock . . .'

His voice trailed off. Trembling all over, the woman was raising her finger. She slowly pointed across the fields to a dark patch of woodland.

That's where they are, Keller thought. *The Nara-Karith are somewhere in there . . .*

11

Dray's snub pistol slipped easily into her hand. Its weight reassured her as she walked across the shadowy border and into the dark woods.

Without her armour weighing her down, her footfalls were light and silent as a fall of ash. Keller and Ayl were trampling twigs to left and right, making a low, constant crackling sound like a hound chewing bones, but there was nothing she could do about that.

The blank, staring eyes of the dead man in the samthorn field kept coming back into her mind. She felt as if they were still watching her. She told herself not to be a superstitious fool, imagining her father's stern voice shouting it as an order.

It helped, but not much.

The tree trunks were vast, the spaces between them cavernous and almost silent. Far overhead, the canopy of leaves rustled with the movements of unseen things.

Snap.

She flinched, but it was only Keller stepping on a large twig. He gave her a pained look of apology. Warily, Dray walked on as the silence closed in on her.

She had no idea what she was walking into. They had to be ready for the Nara-Karith, at the very least. But what else might be waiting with them? In Dray's imagination, every step forward she took might set her foot down on a laceration mine. Every inch they moved could bring them into the sights of Keller's would-be assassin.

She carefully stepped over a tortuously twisted tree root. Nothing stirred.

The assassin had to be a professional, or at least military trained. His shots had been precise. If Dray hadn't had her armour, she'd have been dead. And now she was armourless, exposed. Another shot from that k-gun would blow her ribcage apart like a water balloon—

Squawk!

The sound was halfway between a caw and a shriek. It was right in front of her. Something dark flew up in a wild flurry, beating through the trees.

Dray gave a shrill cry of alarm and opened fire. Two bolts from the snub pistol ripped through the branches.

'Stop!' Keller yelled, grabbing her by the shoulder.

She watched a giant bird-shape go winging off through the trees.

'It's a falchort!' Keller said uneasily. 'You know what a falchort is, right?'

Dray shook her head.

'Just a bird. That's all. It won't hurt us!'

'It was huge!' Dray protested, her body still thrumming with icy adrenalin. 'It was attacking!'

'Attacking?' Keller's broad smile was reassuring and maddening at the same time. 'Falchorts are harmless. We don't have to shoot them, unless you're planning on cooking one, of course. They're good eating.'

Ayl caught up with her. 'Are you all right?'

The concern in his voice just made it worse. Her fighting urge was vanishing. Now Dray just felt humiliated. She'd not only shot at a harmless game bird, she'd yelled like a child afraid of the dark.

Her gun was hot against her leg as she tucked it away. Now her cheeks were growing hot too.

She waved Ayl off. 'I'm fine.'

She knew he had seen the shame burning on her face, because he glanced away to spare her. Kind Ayl. Dray wished harder than ever for her armour, far away in a Cantorian linen cupboard. It would have covered her face, hidden her shame.

She hated to be this exposed. Hated it.

They crept further on, heading deeper into the woods. Dray led the way, not knowing what they were looking for or even if they were heading in the right direction. Occasionally falchorts shrieked their strangled cries from deep in the wooded darkness, but the only other sound was the crick-crackle of footfalls on deep bracken.

When Dray glimpsed the large structure through the trees, she froze. She motioned for the others to stop.

A grey-white crescent of plascrete, it seemed to be waiting to close like a fist on anyone foolish enough to wander into it. Her keen eyes took in details: a transmissions dish, the gunmetal-green mass of fuel tanks, abandoned vehicles below.

'What is it?' Ayl breathed.

'Looks like a miniature spaceport to me,' she guessed. 'One that nobody's supposed to know about. Smugglers, maybe?'

'That's outrageous!' Keller scoffed. 'The Trade Council knows about every ship that goes in and out our atmosphere! Nobody could run a spaceport without Council sanction . . .' His voice trailed off.

Dray nudged Ayl. 'Seems there's a lot going on that Keller doesn't know about, huh?'

'Yeah,' Ayl whispered back. 'And something tells me nobody would have told him even after he was crowned trade king.'

Dray edged closer. There was something huge behind the main structure, not quite concealed. She saw the curve of a hull, a long tailfin, the edge of a manoeuvring jet.

'There's a ship docked here!' she said excitedly.

'Careful,' Keller warned, but she was already moving closer, trying to see more.

The craft, from what she could see, was heavily customized, with non-standard replacement modules crudely welded on. Whoever owned it had cared more about raw power than appearances.

As she gradually skirted the area, the cockpit bubble came into view. It was dark and empty. Something about the ship's outline was naggingly familiar, but she couldn't put her finger on it. The engines had been refitted, she saw, with added fuel pods and an acceleration booster. Whatever this ship had once been, now it seemed like some souped-up smuggler craft.

She moved closer, to where the hatchway stood open. Nearby was a stack of containers, obviously waiting to be loaded on board.

She took a deep breath. 'Hello? Anyone there?'

* * *

Despite the dread he felt as they approached the silent craft, Keller was angry. If this secret port existed, then so did others. The Cantorian officials must be aware of them – and that meant they must be keeping their mouths shut for a good reason. Keller could guess what it was.

Ahead of him, Dray gasped. 'Oh, no!'

'What? What's in there?'

She shook her head. 'This ship – it's a Bellori freighter! Or used to be. It's been heavily modified, but it's one of ours. I knew it looked familiar.' She sighed. 'The hatch controls are labelled in the Bellori alphabet.'

'I know these!' Ayl said, running over to a stack of wire-mesh containers filled with purple fruit. 'These are the fruit I saw the Nara-Karith destroying!'

'Samthorn berries,' said Keller darkly. 'But these aren't destroyed, are they?'

'There's more,' Ayl said, brushing the fallen leaves off another crate. 'Frozen falchort wings.'

'Sacks of flour over here,' Dray said, moving into the shadow under the craft's wing. ' "Produce of Hovah Province", it says. And these are bundles of green things, like roots.'

'They're scrallots,' Keller said, his anger rising.

140

'Cantorian food, like everything else here. All this has been looted from Cantorian farms!'

'Why?' Dray wondered.

'You tell me.'

She rounded on him. 'Are you *accusing* me?'

'This is a Bellori ship!' he yelled back. 'You said so! I got shot at with a Bellori gun! Add it up!'

'What exactly are you saying, Keller?' She was more angry than upset, he could tell. Beside her, Ayl sank to his knees and clutched his head.

'It looks to me like Bellus has been stealing food from Cantor,' Keller said, folding his arms defiantly.

'We would never do anything like that!' She slashed the air with her hand in a vicious gesture of denial. 'If you had any respect for my people, you'd know we never steal!'

'Sure you don't.'

'You slimy Cantorian lowlife . . . stealing is against the Bellori honour code! We'd sooner die than break it!'

Keller heard a rustle from overhead.

Suddenly he was aware just how loud they'd been shouting. Something up there was alert now – and prepared.

Parts of the trees detached themselves and fell like grotesque seed pods. They opened as they fell, unfolding

141

long, thin legs. Sickening thumps came from all around as more and more of the creatures fell from their hiding places.

'Nara-Karith!' Dray yelled.

They had been camouflaged by the leaves, and now they were advancing, scuttling to where the three companions stood in the ship's shadow.

Keller gaped in horror. More Nara-Karith were still falling as the others advanced. There were at least a dozen of them now.

He backed toward the stacked food crates and ducked down beside Dray. 'What the hell do we *do*?'

She dug in her clothing and passed him a reassembled pistol. 'We fight.'

'They're coming!' Ayl wailed. 'The voices . . .'

Keller smacked himself as he realized why Ayl had been clutching his head before. Stupid of him not to see it!

Too late for regrets now. He braced himself, trying to hold the pistol steady.

An ear-piercing screech went up as the Nara-Karith charged.

Keller trained his pistol on the creature bearing down on him and fired three quick bursts, shattering its thorax. It hit the dirt and skidded through the leaves, the body still twitching and clutching reflexively. He shot it again and, with a ghastly final spasm it lay still.

The rest of the creatures swarmed. Beside him, Keller heard Dray's pistol loose burst after burst, and the harsh splattering sounds of Nara-Karith bodies being blown apart. Ayl lay at his feet, whimpering.

Two more of the creatures were advancing on him purposefully, as if they knew what they were doing. They broke into a charge. Keller fired frantically. He couldn't shoot them both in time!

He managed to take out one of the creature's legs, just as the other Nara-Karith crashed down upon him. Crates of food went flying. A claw raked his arm, tearing cloth and drawing blood.

'Dray!' he yelled, fighting to get away from the scrabbling limbs.

She was already there, pistol raised, shielding him.

The Nara-Karith looked up at her, staring right into the barrel of her gun. A sudden blast, and the headless body flew back six paces into the scrub.

Even more of them were falling from the trees now, tumbling down like dislodged spine-nuts.

'There's too many of them,' Keller panted. 'We have to run!'

'Round the back of the ship!' Dray ordered.

Keller dragged Ayl to his feet and followed Dray. She ran between the ship and the spaceport building, heading for the deeper woods.

She stopped suddenly. A line of Nara-Karith were already waiting there, slowly advancing on them.

He looked back. There was a line there too, moving in from behind.

'They've encircled us!' Dray said, horrified. 'While we were fighting, they moved round to the other side. They were never that smart before.' Dray said. 'Oh krack, they're coming—'

'Dray!' Keller screamed, too late. One of the Nara-Karith had scrabbled over the edge of the ship's wing.

She spun around as it launched itself at her. The impact knocked her sprawling.

The thing bit deep into her arm. Dray screamed aloud as blood bubbled up around its mandibles.

Keller watched in horror as it shook her and drew back its claw to land a lethal blow.

The voice in Ayl's mind boomed a chant of hate. *Destroy! Destroy!*

He stood helpless to act, hearing Dray scream, watching her body arch in pain.

Suddenly he was seeing through the Nara-Karith's

144

eyes, looking down at Dray bleeding below him. The creature was going to spear her with its claw, just as another Nara-Karith had killed Trade King Lial.

He felt its raging strength, the burning desire to kill this weak fleshy humanoid. Such tremendous power, but Ayl could feel its brain was simple. It was a beast, obeying orders.

Telepathic orders. But who was giving them?

STOP! he told the Nara-Karith mentally.

He felt it freeze, its claw still raised.

Then its mind became a blinding flash of scarlet pain. Ayl was back in his own head again, looking up at Keller. At the smoking gun in his friend's hand. At the alien collapsed across Dray.

'Here come the rest!' Keller said in a panicked voice, struggling to pull the remains off Dray.

The other Nara-Karith were scuttling in for the kill. Ayl turned and faced them, summoning up all the mental power he could. He focused his mind on the image of a Nara-Karith. He made it as realistic as he could, taking as much time as he dared. He held his hand out towards them.

'Whatever you're doing, Blue, do it fast!' Keller urged.

Ayl held the image in his mind, then broadcast it

out to them, screaming with his thoughts: *DESTROY! DESTROY!*

The Nara-Karith paused, their antennae twitching. Ayl held his breath.

Then they began to attack one another, hacking and slashing with a frenzy that made Ayl feel sick.

He heard Keller's gasp of amazement. 'What the—?'

The fighting was neither quick nor clean. They ripped off each other's limbs and heads, screeching as they did so, making repulsive buzzing, clicking noises.

'Blue,' said Keller in awe. 'What did you do?'

But Ayl didn't answer. He watched in silence as the Nara-Karith tore one another to pieces. Dray coughed, wiping her mouth with a bloodied hand.

Ayl looked at her, concerned, and his concentration broke. Without warning, the Nara-Karith hesitated, as if they were coming to their senses. They began to move in on the attack once more. Ayl quickly sent out the signal again: *Destroy!*

The carnage began again in earnest. Alien blood flew in yellow gouts. They had their orders and they followed them out, like the unthinking drones they were.

When it was all over, and the last of them was a twitching corpse, Ayl let his hand slowly fall. He was exhausted, even more drained than he had been after he'd used telekinesis to move the bolts of fabric.

'That was all of them, I think,' he said huskily. 'They're dead. They were following orders to attack us, but I-I-I forced them to kill each other.'

'You saved our lives, is what you did!' said Keller.

Something caught Ayl's eye. He looked over at the sprawled remains of the Nara-Karith that had fallen on Dray. Its mouth was smeared with her blood. Had it twitched? Probably just a reflex—

It lurched up and staggered towards him.

Not dead. Keller had just stunned it!

Its jaws parted, descending upon his face.

He threw up his arms and screamed.

The sound mingled with the roar of Dray's pistol.

The Nara-Karith's head, inches from his own, exploded like an overripe fruit. The shower of yellow fluids caught Ayl full in the face, splashing over him in a stinking rain.

His hands were dripping with blood, just like before. He stared down at them, feeling no revulsion, just a deep, grim satisfaction that he was alive and it was dead.

What am I becoming? he thought to himself. *Is this the end of the nightmare – or the beginning?*

12

Keller ripped a long strip of fabric from his shirt and began to wrap it carefully around Dray's wounded arm.

'You should scorch it,' Dray said hoarsely. 'Keep it from getting infected.'

'I don't think so,' Keller said.

She punched him weakly. 'Soft-hearted Cantorian.' He tightened the bandage and she sucked air through her teeth. Her face twisted in a grimace.

'Sorry,' he said.

'It's not that,' she told him. 'I just . . . I can't believe we fell for it!'

That puzzled him. 'Fell for what?'

'It's a classic Bellori battle strategy,' she explained, sitting up. 'Encirclement. You appear weak in one direction to get the enemy to move there, then you close the net on them. We've been doing it ever since . . .' She shrugged. 'Ever since we fought with pointed sticks and rocks, I think.'

'They definitely seemed smarter,' Keller agreed. 'It was creepy.'

'Just being more intelligent wouldn't teach them new tactics, though,' Dray said. 'Encirclement takes training, discipline. Ayl said they were following orders – do you think someone could have taught them?' The thought made goose-flesh rise on her arms.

'Nara-Karith . . . with specialist battle moves?' wondered Keller. 'Maybe they have a new queen?'

'Hey!' Ayl yelled from inside the ship. 'You're going to want to have a look at this!'

As they headed up the ramp and into the craft's cluttered hold, Dray realized she hadn't even noticed Ayl slipping away into the ship. Either Ayl had been quiet for a surprisingly long time – or Dray had been too focused on her arm to notice anything else.

'Talk to us, Blue,' said Dray. 'What've you found?'

Ayl held up a data slate. He was still plastered with yellow blood, Dray saw – more so than any of them. 'Ship's log,' he announced. 'It was docked with the main nav console here.'

'So what is this ship?' Keller asked. 'Who owns it? Where's it come from?'

'Seems to come from all over,' Ayl said. 'It's been travelling from one planet to another for weeks now.

Take a look.'

Dray and Keller bent over the slate, watching the glowing data unfold across the screen. Spinning planets in wireframe zoomed in and out as the data slate relived the ship's journeys.

Dray read the planets' names out one by one. 'Galufrac. Orgren. Manax 3.' None of them meant anything to her. 'Pellucia. Arat. Anyone?'

'Orgren!' Ayl said, snapping his fingers. 'I've heard that name before. When I was reading minds in the market.' He hesitated. 'The guy was a mess. All he could think about was getting away from the "spiders" who destroyed his planet. It's a safe bet Orgren was overrun by the Nara-Karith.'

'There's its last stop.' Keller poked a finger at the screen. 'Some chunk of rock called Zarix, moon of Gimruth 4.' He frowned. 'What's the deal? There's nothing out there. It's leagues away from anywhere.'

'Krack,' Dray said, feeling suddenly cold. Her wounded arm ached like frozen wires were being twisted in the flesh. 'I heard my father talking about Zarix on the way to Cantor. It's one of our bases. We've lost some patrols there.'

'Lost?' Ayl looked incredulous. 'You mean, they were destroyed?'

'No, lost contact. They just went silent. I tried to get more out of my father, but he wouldn't tell me anything.' Dray glanced around the ship, uncomfortable now in its dark hollow spaces. Knowing that this craft had likely been involved in the loss of Bellori patrols made her feel deeply uneasy.

'There's something happening on Zarix!' Keller said. 'The Nara-Karith, this ship, your lost patrols, it's all got to be connected!'

'We need to be sure. And there's only one way to do that,' Dray said. 'If we could fly this thing, override the controls somehow . . .'

Keller was already prising open the instrument panel.

'Cross your fingers, everyone . . .'

Keller twisted two very different-looking wires together. A deep fizz came from somewhere inside the ship.

Next moment the console flared into life, instrument panels coming online one by one like illuminating jewels and display screens flicking from dusty grey-black into glaring neon blue.

'Come on,' he told Dray. 'Don't tell me you're not impressed.'

She wrinkled her nose. 'You'd never manage that with a *proper* Bellori ship. Security circuits would fry you. Anyway, we're not off the ground yet.'

Ayl came back into the cabin. 'I checked the whole ship, top to bottom. No Nara-Karith on board anywhere.'

'Good,' said Keller. 'I don't fancy the idea of fighting those things in space again. Not after the last time.' He took the pilot's chair. 'Dray, can you get on the nav console? Ayl – nothing personal, but maybe clean that blood off yourself? It smells a bit.'

He pressed the control to activate the engines, thinking *Don't blow up, please don't blow up*.

There was a moment of silence, then the slow rising whine of the ship firing up and the turbines starting to spin. He grinned broadly.

'Let's burn,' he said, and pulled the main drive throttle.

The whole ship groaned as the customized drive blasted it straight up like a shot from a cannon. Enormous G-forces dragged at their cheeks before the ship's grav system realized what was happening and compensated automatically.

'Do we need to go so fast?' Ayl protested. 'We'll burn to a cinder!'

'Look at the readouts!' yelled Dray. 'All the friction from the atmosphere! The outer hull's practically on fire!'

'That's the idea,' Keller yelled over the noise. 'Burn off anything clinging to the ship!'

He pointed at a monitor, showing a shaky view of Cantor's landscape retreating into the distance. As they watched, something scorched and barely recognisable fell tumbling, its legs still spasming.

'Good thinking,' Dray said quietly. 'And I thought you were just being a boy racer.'

'How are those things back?' Ayl wondered. 'That's what I don't understand. I thought we destroyed all of them when the asteroid exploded.'

'Maybe some of them got away?' Dray offered. 'You know how tough they are. They could survive in space for a long, long time.'

'One or two, maybe,' said Keller. 'But we just saw *twenty* of the kracking things. And Orgren was completely overrun, like Ayl said.'

'So maybe there was more than one asteroid,' Ayl suggested. 'Fish don't lay just one egg, do they? What if the asteroid was just one fragment of something much bigger?'

It wasn't a comforting thought. 'There could be

thousands out there,' said Keller. 'Or millions.'

'That's going to take a lot of killing,' Dray murmured.

To Keller's surprise, Ayl nodded. He didn't even protest.

'You OK, Blue?' he asked carefully. 'I know you guys don't . . . well, don't really *do* fighting. Is this—'

'I'm fine,' Ayl said in a flat voice. 'It's strange. The killing, the violence … it isn't making me ill like it used to. I hate it, but I have to live with it.' He paused, looking at his hands. 'And I can do more, now, with these new powers of mine. I can help you guys and make a difference.'

'And we're out of the atmosphere!' Keller announced, glad to change the subject. Through the cockpit bubble, the blue haze of Cantor's stratosphere was receding, giving way to black infinity. 'Ready to make the jump to Zarix, as soon as Dray lays in a course.'

Dray was muttering harshly at the console and thumping it. 'Useless piece of . . .' Keys clicked. 'No use. It won't link up to the Bellori data hub!'

'Ah. We should maybe have expected that,' Keller said. 'This ship doesn't look like it's been Bellori property for a while.'

'May as well head back to Cantor!' Dray kicked the

154

terminal angrily. 'We can't lock our course without a live link.'

'How come?' asked Ayl.

'The ship's computer needs an up-to-date information stream to calculate the jump safely,' Dray explained, obviously struggling to keep her temper.

'Why?' Ayl frowned. 'What's unsafe about jumping? Can't computers predict where planets are going to be?'

'Planets, yes,' Dray said. 'But not other ships or random stuff like wormholes. The further you jump, the riskier it gets. That's why we have the data hub. It pulls in information from all over.'

'So let's override the computer and do it the old-fashioned way,' Keller said. 'Lots of little jumps instead of one big one.'

Dray goggled at Keller. 'You're going to *star-hop*?'

'That's right. Get the charts out. It'll be fun.'

Half an hour later, Ayl realized that star-hopping was anything but fun. They were seven jumps into the journey, dangerously close to a red giant, and not where they were supposed to be.

Ayl had a pounding headache – but it was from Keller and Dray's squabbling rather than the Nara-Karith. Keller had wanted to hop from star to star down the spine of the Devonis Cluster. Dray had insisted that they would all die if they tried that because the central star was about to go nova, and the obvious course was via Pratchett's Beacon.

Keller had followed his own instincts, but Ayl wasn't convinced that his friend had made the right choice.

'Head for that blue one up there, on the right!' Dray said. 'That's the Fellstar. It'll get us back on course.'

'We're already orbiting the kracking Fellstar!' Keller yelled. 'I'm jumping to Thrakol next!'

Dray shuffled the star charts. 'Frakol? That's back the other way, towards Galactic Central Point! You want to head for Panolasca.'

'Not Frakol. Thrakol!'

'Chill out, guys,' said Ayl. 'Arguing isn't helping anything.'

Keller slammed the lever forward for the next jump. The ship thrummed all over, the engines screamed, and everything did a wibbly-wobbly blurred dance that reminded Ayl of swimming through a school of electric kallins.

Then the stars were crystallising around them again, the ship came back into focus, and they were somewhere new. Twin suns burned in front of them, casting an arc of rainbow light into the cockpit.

'It's beautiful!' Ayl whispered.

'I don't care!' Keller shouted, ramping up the engines again. 'It can be as beautiful as it kracking likes! The point is, *we're not where we're supposed to be*!'

They jumped.

And found themselves in void space, with no stars nearby at all.

'Maybe if we jump back to the Fellstar,' Dray suggested, 'but this time go spinwards, out to Pandorica Major . . .'

'I'm not sure that even was the Fellstar back there, to be honest,' Keller admitted, sagging in defeat. 'We're lost, plain and simple.'

Suddenly, Ayl doubled over as relentless, piercing shrieks filled his head.

'Oh come on, Blue, don't be so dramatic,' said Dray, disapprovingly.

'It's the voices,' Ayl groaned. 'The Nara-Karith. I can hear them . . .'

Dray sprang up. 'On the ship?'

'No!' Ayl waved a hand at the starry void. 'Out . . . there.'

A hopeful look crossed Keller's face. 'Where exactly? Point to where the voices are coming from.'

Ayl hesitated, then pointed out at nothingness, in

the direction of the horrible voices. Keller swivelled the ship around, made a here-goes-nothing face and threw the ship into a jump.

They re-emerged into normal space and Ayl winced. '*Ai*. OK. Now they're louder. A lot louder!' He pointed again. 'That's where they are!'

Once again, Keller jumped. As the ship settled back down into normal space, Dray's navigation console made a dull chiming sound.

'I think we've arrived!' she said. 'The computer's showing that something's out there . . .'

Her voice trailed off.

Clutching his head, Ayl stared out at the vast, dead moon that had come into view ahead, looming out of space like the skeletal remains of some earlier universe.

13

'Bring us in!' Dray urged Keller. 'I want to see what's down there.'

'Hold on just a sec. Blue? You know that stealth field thing you did, back when we were heading to the asteroid?'

Ayl nodded. 'You mean the cloaking field? Do you want me to do it again?'

'Yeah. Think you can manage it?'

'I expect so. Let me concentrate.' Ayl settled himself cross-legged at the front of the cockpit, looking out through the bubble. He laid his hands on his knees and closed his eyes.

Keller waited, rocked back and forth in his chair and drummed his fingers on the console.

Ayl held up a hand. 'Don't do that, please.'

'Sorry,' Keller said, sitting still.

'It's OK. I just need to concentrate.'

Eventually Ayl nodded in satisfaction, saying,

'There. Anyone looking our way should see nothing but empty space. Even the scanners won't pick us up.'

'Good one,' Keller said. 'OK, people, hold on to your hats. We're going in.'

He racked the ship's impulse drives up to full thrust and entered the atmosphere. Turbulence buffeted the craft and an ominous groaning noise came from the hull.

'Don't shake us apart!' Dray warned.

'She'll hold together,' Keller promised. The moon's surface was visible beneath them now, a miserable panorama of lava plains and craggy mountains, with scuds of filthy-looking cloud seething over it.

'What a dump!' he murmured. 'What in hell would bring anyone out here?'

'Punishment?' Ayl suggested, peering down into the violent windstorm.

'I guess it could be used as a prison, or something,' Keller mused. 'But I expect most people would prefer death.'

He brought the ship even lower, skating through the thin atmosphere, staying well above the mountain peaks. This ship was tough, but those razor-sharp rocks would gut it like a fish.

'I already told you why my people are here,' Dray said, sounding a little annoyed. 'It's a strategic military outpost, not a holiday camp. We have deep scanners here, keeping watch over this part of the galaxy. All so that Cantorians and Aquanths can sleep easily in their beds.'

'We don't actually use beds,' Ayl pointed out. 'Some of us like to sleep among shara-weeds, though. They leak out chemicals that freshen you up . . .' He realized Dray wasn't listening, and stopped.

'Getting a signal from up ahead!' Keller said. 'Should be able to magnify the source . . . there. Putting it up on the main viewscreen now.'

The hazy, static-plagued image of a landed ship appeared. Dark figures, almost impossible to make out, were standing in battle formation beside it.

'That ship!' Dray yelled instantly. 'It's a Bellori Firehawk!'

'Is that so odd? You said this is a Bellori base,' said Keller.

'Yeah, but a Firehawk's a *warship*! See the troops? Usually there's only a crew of technicians on a listening post like this. That ship must have been sent here to find out what happened to the other patrols!'

Ayl flinched at her jarringly loud voice, muttered

161

something, and frowned in redoubled concentration.

'Makes sense,' Keller agreed. 'Keep that cloak going, Ayl. I'll bring us in closer.'

'Look!' Dray said, dismayed. Where the Bellori were gathered, staccato flashes of light were detonating.

Keller knew what that meant. Gunfire. The Bellori were under attack!

'Get us in there, Keller!' Dray said through clenched teeth. 'That's my people getting chewed up down there. *Move!*'

'I'm doing my best!' Keller muttered. 'We'll be there in under a minute . . . less, if I can pull it off.'

Dray turned back to the viewscreen. The image was clearer now that they were closing the distance. The Bellori were kneeling, taking cover behind rocks and throwing grenades.

Keller expanded the image. For the first time, Dray got a clear view of what was attacking the troops. Horrified, she uttered a Bellori curse. Beside her, Ayl gasped aloud.

There were ranks of Nara-Karith advancing on the soldiers, organized into a formation like a V. Bellori rifle fire and grenade explosions ripped through their numbers, but no sooner was one alien riven to

162

bits than another took its place.

'They're using tactics again!' she insisted, banging the console in frustration. 'That's a classic armoured wedge! How have they learned to fight like that?'

'Hold on. I'm hearing telepathic orders,' Ayl said, one slim hand on his forehead. 'Gamma Wing is being told to . . . disengage and fall back for recuperation.' He made a pained face. 'I can't focus on two things at once.'

'Who's giving the orders?' asked Dray. She would sever this army's head if she got the chance.

'I can't tell! They're being relayed from one Nara-Karith to another. No way to listen in on the original source!'

'So keep listening!' Dray urged. 'Tell us what they're saying!'

'What good will that do from up here?' Keller complained. She ignored him.

'Zeta Wing, break formation and flank left,' Ayl recited. 'Omega Wing, break formation and flank right. Incarcerate enemy . . .'

'That's a pincer move!' Dray screamed at the Bellori on the screen. 'Get out of there! They're flanking you – they'll tear into you from both sides!'

The Nara-Karith were already breaking the Bellori

battle line. Dray raged and shouted orders that none of the soldiers could hear.

The monsters began to swarm over the Bellori troops. Dray watched them being flung into rocks, caught out by the surprise tactics.

Keller and Ayl said nothing. The roar of the ship's engines, strained to overloading point, filled the cabin.

'My people,' she said, her voice hoarse and small. 'They're cutting them down like samthorn trees.'

'Look,' Keller said. 'They're rounding them up.'

'To slaughter them!' Dray said angrily. 'While we watch!' The thought of her kinsmen being murdered, unarmed and defenceless, made her half-insane with anger. It was dishonour, the worst of insults.

'I don't think so.' Keller pointed. The Nara-Karith were binding up the soldiers' wrists and ankles. 'They're taking prisoners.'

'We're close!' Ayl said excitedly. 'Look at the screens – we're right above them!'

Keller brought the ship to a standstill. They all looked out of the cockpit to where the battle was taking place in reality.

The sight of so many Nara-Karith made Dray ache for a fusion bomb. She could wipe them all out in one glorious, cindery second.

But a bomb would kill Bellori soldiers as well. A rescue would have to do. She went to the hatchway controls and stood, irritably waiting for the ship to drop.

'Land the ship!' she ordered. 'What are you waiting for?'

Keller shook his head. 'I'm sorry, Dray. I won't do that.'

'What? What is *wrong* with you?'

Dray's furious shout made Ayl flinch. He focused his thoughts on the psychic shield keeping them hidden. So long as he concentrated, they would stay invisible – but Dray wasn't making it easy.

She grabbed Keller by the collar, practically spitting in his face. 'My people are getting torn to bits down there, and you won't land?'

'Get a grip on yourself!' Keller yelled back, grabbing her wrists and shoving her away from him. 'Have you seen how many of those things are down there? We're worse than outnumbered!'

'But we've got surprise on our side! We can turn things around, we can help!'

Keller stood between Dray and the controls. 'It's

165

insane! Do you want to charge in and die? Is that your idea of a glorious death in battle?'

'You've given up before the fight's even started!' Dray snarled. 'You'd take us down there if you had any stomach at all!' She sneered and prodded him above the waistband. 'Stomach for a *fight*, that is.'

Ayl realized he wasn't focusing on the shield. The argument was too distracting. In panic, he jerked his mind back to the stealth bubble.

He kept it from collapsing, but only just.

'Do you two have to do this *now*?' he said through clenched teeth.

Keller spoke to Dray slowly and deliberately, though he was shaking with anger. 'One: it's suicide, not bravery. Two: they don't know we're here, we'd be throwing that away. Three: we don't know *anything* about what or who is controlling them. I know it's hard, most of all for you, but we have to stay hidden, we have to learn as much as we can. Then we can intervene. Not before.'

Dray looked at him with contempt. 'Do you know what we say on Bellus about people like you? "All jawbone, no backbone." You'd say anything if it got you out of having to fight. Because you're a coward.'

Ayl swallowed. He knew Dray had just hurled the

worst insult a Bellori could give. By the looks of him, Keller knew it too.

'Come on, Dray,' said Ayl pleadingly. 'You know you don't really mean that. Let's just take a step back and calm down.'

'Butt out, Blue!' she snapped. 'Don't you start going wet on me too.'

Keller folded his arms. 'You're way out of line, Dray. Sit down.'

'Get out of the way, Keller. I'll land this ship myself if I have to.'

Ayl rubbed his aching eyes. He could barely keep his mind on the stealth field.

'Do I have to spell it out to you?' Keller yelled back. 'We. Have. Not. Got. A. Plan. Charging in without any kind of strategy isn't heroic, it's stupid!'

'So we think on our feet, use our initiative!'

'Shut up!' Ayl yelled. 'Both of you, shut up! I can't keep us hidden if I can't concentrate!' He was breathing hard and clutching his head.

'Oh, krack,' said Keller, sitting down heavily in the pilot's chair. 'Ayl, I'm sorry, I didn't think.'

'It's too late,' Ayl groaned. 'I think I lost it.'

'Get the field back up!' Dray said urgently. 'We'll keep quiet, just get it—'

There was a thunderous *whump* as something smashed into the ship.

'We've been hit!' Keller shouted.

14

'What was it?' Dray gasped. 'A missile?'

Keller pointed at the ship's transparent frontal canopy. 'No. That!'

The thing clambering into view on segmented legs was worse than any missile. Vast and hideous, it clung to the outside of the ship like a grotesque parasite.

It was a Nara-Karith, but like none they had ever seen before. Easily three times the size of the others, it all but covered the cockpit bubble and blotted out their view of the planet completely.

'What the Great Abyss is that thing?' Ayl stammered.

Its arms unfolded, displaying claws like scythe blades. To Keller's horror, it began to tear deep gashes in the ship's outer hull. Metal screeched and armour plate sheared back like paper.

Foam anti-vacuum sealant spurted out of the holes and hardened, as if the ship were bleeding. One of its claws snagged an outer module and tore it off in a

169

shower of sparks. With a sudden blast of static, the viewscreen went dead.

Keller cursed. 'It's like it knew where to hit us!'

The creature lowered its head and stared in at them. With one leg it pounded at the transparent surface, creating a white constellation of cracks.

'It's armoured!' Ayl said, pointing at the thing's thorax. It was like a horrible parody of a Bellori warrior. Scaled plates had been grafted on to the creature's body, leaving holes for the legs.

'What the—?' screamed Dray in stark disbelief. 'That's Bellori armour plating! Where did that come from?'

'This isn't like the others,' Ayl warned, mental strain showing on his face. He looked exhausted enough to faint. 'The brain . . . more complex . . .'

The creature's jaws champed at the canopy, blearing it with drool and scoring marks on to the surface. Keller got a sickening glimpse into its pulsing gullet. It made him queasy to think there was nothing between it and him but that thin transparent layer, now marred and scratched all over.

'Keller, I can't control its thoughts!' Ayl yelled. 'It's going to smash its way in!'

'Buckle up!' Keller yelled. He fastened himself into

the pilot's seat, not bothering to check whether the others had done the same. He switched the engines from hover to thrust.

He and Dray were flung back in their seats as the acceleration hit. Ayl hadn't reached his chair in time and was hurled, yelling, to the back of the bridge.

Flying blind, Keller thought, with a rueful glance at the dead viewscreen. *Can't even see through the canopy with that thing in the way. Just going to have to trust my instincts.*

The creature raised its two limbs and scrabbled at the clear polymer, criss-crossing it with white lines. That left only four arms to hold on with. Crossing his fingers, Keller activated the airbrakes and hit full retro thrust.

Dray was almost slammed out of her seat. Ayl went tumbling across the floor, caught hold of the seat fastening and clung on. Keller's own seat harness caught him like a body blow, winding him.

He looked up. The enormous Nara-Karith was dangling by one claw, not quite dislodged, scrabbling feverishly to regain its grip.

'Just die, won't you!' Keller yelled. He threw the ship into a tight barrel roll, hoping it would throw the monster off and send it plummeting to its death. The force of the spin was sickening, bringing bile into his mouth. He heard one of the engines give a spluttering choked roar, as if something had been sucked into it.

As he righted the ship again, he saw the thing was gone from the bubble, leaving only a streak of yellow. He was about to punch the air and yell in triumph when he saw the spider-like limbs clambering back across the bubble, followed by the head. One of the arms had been torn off, but the creature was still coming.

He swung the ship violently from one side to the other, but it clung on. It slammed its head down on the bubble and, with a terrible splintering crunch, a long crack appeared.

'I can't shake it off!' he yelled.

Dray punched her harness clasp and leapt out of her seat. She pulled herself up the short ladder to the ship's turret, powered up the laser cannons and took aim. Keller heard her grunt 'Eat this, you lump of—'

The cannons fired, lighting up the outside of the ship in a citrine flare. Keller saw the bolts strike the thing full in the body. Surely it couldn't survive that?

The glare faded, and he saw the still-glowing patch on the thing's Bellori armour. It had survived a full blast from a ship-mounted weapon.

'You just made it really angry,' Ayl gasped from under his chair. 'I can hear what it's thinking. It's going to rip you apart. Dray, I can't stop it, *get out of that turret!*'

Dray dropped down as the Nara-Karith came stalking across the outer hull in her direction. There was a groan and creak as something metallic was bent out of place.

'Is it tearing off our guns?' Dray asked in horror.

Just then, there was a terrific grinding, tearing sound, like old rusty gates being forced open, followed by an abrupt bang. The whole ship lurched sideways and sagged. Alarm klaxons were howling and a red light was frantically flashing on Keller's console.

He stared at it, unable to believe what it was telling him. 'We just lost a wing,' he said hollowly.

Hurricane winds thrummed around the ship as it began to fall. Keller gripped the joystick tightly, fighting to keep them level.

'Can you land?' Dray said, struggling to keep her footing.

'I'll try!' Keller promised.

The horizon outside veered even further out of kilter as the ship went into a roll. Keller wrestled with controls that jerked crazily in his grip. So long as they had power he could still manoeuvre, but he knew there was precious little chance of a safe landing now.

They were going to crash. He was dead certain of it. All he could do was try to crash somewhere broad, open and flat . . .

Ayl had always hated flying. It was so different from the weightless ease of water, where you could swim up, down and around without ever worrying about gravity. Up in the merciless empty air, gravity was always waiting to drag you down to your death like a devouring kraken.

The swivel post fixing his chair to the floor was cold black metal. He clung on to it, trusting it with his life. It had been the first thing within grabbing reach when the ship had braked suddenly. Now it was his anchor in the storm, the only one he had. He was so tired, drained from the effort of keeping the shield up, but he forced his muscles to obey.

'You can still land, right?' he shouted.

'We've still got thrust!' Keller called back. 'So we can fire the lifters as an airbrake. We'll come down hard, but we should make it!'

Ayl could see the horizon rocking wildly as Keller did his best to steady the ship. At least that creature wasn't blocking the canopy any more. With a cold shock, Ayl realized he hadn't heard the thing moving around since it had torn the wing off.

That meant it was busy somewhere.

Where had it gone? Had the mad pitching flung it off? Maybe it had abandoned the ship, thinking they were doomed to crash and die. Ayl hoped so.

The floor vibrated beneath him. He clung tightly to the chair post, fighting to keep the terror out of his mind.

A resounding crash came from the rear of the ship. There was a crack-hiss of escaping gases. Metal tore and pinions gave way.

Keller swore. 'Oh this is bad, this is bad, this is—'

Then the noise stopped. The other sounds around them steadily died away to an eerie near-silence. They were coasting silently through nothingness. Only the shrill whistling of the wind over the ship's hull remained.

Ayl knew the lack of noise was not a good thing, but his exhausted brain couldn't remember why.

Then the full horror of it struck him. *He could no longer hear the ship's engine.*

'We've lost engine power.' Keller flicked switches frantically, to no effect. 'Going into freefall – can't hold it!'

Ayl braced himself. This was it. The end.

All his life he had been taught that death was merely another stage on life's journey, a change to be understood and accepted, not feared. Now those teachings seemed like empty noise.

He was going to die. And he couldn't lie to himself any more. He was terrified. He didn't want to die, not now, not ever.

Wind screamed outside, and there came the clang-clang-clang of the creature moving back across the hull.

'Impact in sixty clicks,' Keller said, punching a toggle. 'Come on, backups, *fire!*'

Ayl forced himself to recite the Chant of Life's Ending. That was what you were meant to do when you knew death was coming.

'*Kha me lo careliaa, kha me lo careliaa . . .*'

He suddenly remembered being four turns old, hearing his grandfather recite that same chant on his deathbed. The old eyes, rolled back into the withered skull. He'd been frightened.

Ayl hadn't thought of that moment in many long turns. More memories were surging up like bubbles – his mother's investiture as high priestess . . . the time he'd been stung by the prism geloid . . . the way his friend Wan had waited outside his hospital pod and

176

refused to leave . . .

Ayl closed his eyes and kept chanting.

'Impact in thirty clicks!' Keller yelled. 'Dray, watch out!'

Unbelievably, the huge Nara-Karith in armour was back, attacking the cockpit bubble with vicious force. In three quick brutal cracks, it was through. Freezing winds rushed into the bridge as the thing tore the remaining fragments away.

It crawled on to the bridge. Ayl looked up at it looming over him.

'Ten clicks!' Keller screamed, hauling back on the joystick. 'Nine, eight . . .'

The gigantic brute raised a spear-like forelimb. For one horrendous moment, Ayl wondered if his fate was to be impaled or killed in a crash. From close by came a clack-click as Dray unclipped a plasma rifle from its mount.

'Smile, you ugly scum-sucker,' she grunted.

The bridge lit up as Dray blasted the thing from point-blank range.

Ayl heard it screech, smelled its burning flesh. He heard Dray screaming curses, and the deafening howl of the wind, rising to an ungodly roar and obliterating everything.

He stammered a prayer. Something snatched him off the floor. A firm pressure was on his mouth.

The creature's got me, he thought. *Please let this be quick.*

Thunder.

And darkness.

Dray's first waking thought was: *At least I went down fighting, my weapon in my hand. Good. That's how a Bellori should die.*

Her second was, *Hold on – if I'm dead, how come I'm thinking this?*

She was floating, weightless, like a disembodied spirit. An oxygen mask was pressed over her face. When she looked down, she didn't see her own body as she'd half expected. There was only the buckled wreckage of the ship's bridge. Whatever force was keeping her suspended, it had kept her away from a messy death.

Then she understood.

It's the ship's gelfield!

All Bellori ships had them – powerful field emitters that cushioned the crew in bubbles of invisible force in the event of a crash landing. Already she could feel herself drifting to the floor, unhurt. She pulled off the mask and breathed the thin, icy air.

What remained of the bridge was in near-total darkness, lit only by the spark-crackling end of a severed cable. They must have hit the ground like a missile, because a mound of ashen-grey dirt had crammed itself through the opening where the canopy had been.

There was no sign of the Nara-Karith creature.

Keller and Ayl emerged from the shadows, looking shaken. 'How are we still alive?' Keller asked. 'I was sure I was dead!'

'Me too,' Ayl said. 'I've never prayed so hard in my life, and we Aquanths pray *a lot*.'

Dray grinned. 'Bellori safety features,' she said. 'Best designs in the galaxy.'

'Remind me to invest in the company that makes them,' Keller said. 'I'll give them the royal seal of approval!'

Dray found an emergency lightstick and ignited it. The greenish-yellow glow made the wrecked bridge look like some ghoulish, haunted underworld.

'What the heck was that bug, anyway?' she wondered. 'It wasn't like the others. It was way bigger, for one thing.'

'A mutant?' guessed Ayl. 'Maybe some sort of super-drone?'

'Could be. But that wouldn't explain the Bellori

armour it was wearing.' She frowned in thought. 'Someone fitted that on to it, just like someone taught the others to follow military commands.'

'You're unbelievable,' Keller said with a soft laugh. 'We just survived a crash that could have splattered us across a ten kilopace crater, and do you waste any time celebrating? No, you're straight back in action!'

Dray laughed too. She *was* glad to be alive, and to see her friends safe too. 'Can't help it. It's just the way I'm wired.'

Next moment, the mound of earth exploded. The huge Nara-Karith clawed its way out of the dirt that had buried it, hissing and roaring. Dray lunged for the plasma rifle, but an arm grabbed her round the middle and hoisted her off the ground.

'Get off!' she screamed, hammering with her fists at the thing's leathery skin. It took no notice, pausing only to snatch up Keller and Ayl in two more of its arms. Then it headed for the blocked opening that had been the ship's frontal canopy. Ignoring their shouts and cries, it began to dig with its two remaining limbs. The stump of the sixth flexed and oozed in a way that made Dray feel faintly sick.

An idea came to her. She took a breath and bellowed, 'I am Dray, daughter of General Iccus, commander-in-chief of the Bellori! You know who the Bellori are, don't you? So if you value your life – let us GO!'

The creature showed no sign of having understood her, or even of having heard. It dragged them through the narrow opening it had dug, scraping their limbs painfully against the gritty earth.

Then they were out, being carried over the rocky surface of Zarix under a dead black sky. The thin atmosphere hurt Dray's lungs and the chill bit deep into her flesh. Even for a Bellori, disdainful of comfort, this place was grim.

'Didn't you hear me, you brainless bug?' She kicked it as hard as she could.

'It doesn't know who General Iccus is,' said Ayl wearily. 'All it's thinking about are its orders. "Capture intruders, return to base." '

'So where is its base?' Keller wondered.

Dray saw a low, fortified building coming into view up ahead. An armoured command dome sat on top of it, bristling with automated weapons.

'They're using our barracks!' she said, feeling like her hatred for the Nara-Karith could grow no worse. 'They steal our armour, they kill our soldiers . . . and now they infest our base?'

'Well . . . there is one . . . positive side to all this,'

said Keller, struggling in the giant bug's vice-like grip.

'There is?' asked Dray. The creature was hauling them into the barracks now. 'What?'

'We might finally get some answers.'

The Nara-Karith hauled them up a winding spiral ramp, through a warren of corridors and dumped them unceremoniously on a cold stone floor. They were in the heart of the command dome, facing a long wall of computer terminals and scanner screens. Only one of the seats was occupied, by a single enormous figure in Bellori armour with its back to them.

'How nice to see you again,' came the rumble of a deep voice as the figure turned to face them.

Dray knew that voice only too well.

'Sudor!' she snarled.

15

'Welcome to Zarix!' Sudor boomed, spreading his arms wide. 'You've come a long, long way from your precious Trinity System! Tell me, how was your journey? Not too eventful, I hope?'

'Nothing we couldn't handle,' Keller said. He was damned if he'd show fear to this gloating warmonger.

Sudor gave a low, sinister chuckle. 'Is that so. I suggest you make yourselves comfortable, since the ship you stole isn't going anywhere for quite some time. A pity; I spent a lot of time customising that vessel. So. Let's have a little chat.'

He leaned back in his seat and pressed some controls on his wrist. The beeping, chattering terminals behind him became silent; only their flickering lights revealed they were still active.

'There, that's better. It's so nice to see you children again. Look at you all! Growing up so fast!'

'What in hell are you doing here, Sudor?' Dray hissed.

He waved her question away with a gauntleted hand. 'All in good time, my dear. Sit down and behave yourself like a good girl. Tell me, do you like my new friends?'

A door at the end of the hall hissed open, and another of the huge Nara-Karith creatures entered. Its head brushed the ceiling and the Bellori armour over its carapace was neatly fitted, as if it had been made to order.

'Can I offer you some refreshment?' he asked.

The creature reached out a claw and grasped a metal nutri-broth cylinder. As it crossed the room towards Keller, the claw sliced through the metal and the two halves fell with a ringing peal. Hot liquid spilled across the floor and lay there steaming.

Keller stepped out of the way. The creature had just sliced through a reinforced steel, heavy-duty military food container as if it had been soft cheese.

Sudor shook his head sadly. 'What a pity. My friends don't know their own strength. I'm afraid you will have to go hungry.'

'Like you didn't plan for that to happen,' Keller said cynically. 'We get it. Those things are tough. One just tore that ship apart, remember?'

'Mmm. I do hope you're impressed. If not, I can arrange a more *personal* demonstration,' Sudor said dangerously. He snapped his fingers and the creature scuttled closer. A drop of its saliva fell on to Keller's shirtfront, and he wiped it off with distaste.

'I call them my Meta-Karith!' Sudor said proudly. 'A new, bigger, better breed! They are as superior to the ordinary Nara-Karith in combat as a Bellori warrior is to a flabby Cantorian brat like you.'

'Don't mind him, Keller,' said Dray. 'He's not much of a Bellori warrior himself. How are those bruises I gave you, Sudor? Healing well?'

Sudor snarled and made as if to strike her, but Ayl asked a question that turned his head. 'This new breed – you made them yourself, didn't you?'

'At least one of you has a smattering of intelligence,' Sudor murmured. 'Yes. I traced the Nara-Karith asteroid to its point of origin, and found clutches of eggs drifting in the void . . . *thousands* of them, still fertile! I used experimental nutrients to nourish a few of the largest larvae and expand their brains. Then it was just a matter of baiting the trap.' He laughed thickly. 'My mighty creatures required the strongest armour in the galaxy, and a few dead Bellori patrols provided that!'

Dray looked like she was about to spit in his face.

Keller thought to himself: *He found the eggs, but we destroyed the queen. So unless he's got some more eggs stashed away, he can't make any more Nara-Karith!*

'So, what, do we call you now? King of the Spiders?' he asked disgustedly.

'So sorry to have intruded on *your* little coronation,' Sudor sneered back. He mimed taking aim with a rifle and firing. 'Shocking behaviour. I'm sure I won't be invited back. Will you ever forgive me, Your Royal Highness?'

That came as a shock. But Keller had to struggle to keep the expression of hatred on his face. He felt strangely relieved to find out that the assassin had been Sudor. Even though many of his subjects hated him, none of them had hated him enough to try to kill him.

That meant there was still time. There was still hope. But first, he had to deal with Sudor . . .

'So it was you in the purple robe,' Keller said offhandedly. 'Bad choice. Purple really isn't your colour.'

'Really?' Sudor mused. 'I thought you looked very kingly in red. I wanted to see you *dripping* with red.'

'Why try to kill him?' Dray demanded.

'To cause a distraction, of course, you idiots!' Sudor leapt from his chair and began to pace up and down. 'The entire Trinity System will pay for my dishonour!

186

These creatures you see are only the vanguard of my army. I have more, oh yes!'

'You defiled our dead,' said Dray, caught between amazement and hate. 'You are beyond redemption, Sudor. You are no longer Bellori. There is no word for what you are!'

'Shut up, brat,' Sudor snapped. 'There is a simple word for what I am. *Superior*. I am the avenging flame of fate! My creations are the perfect army – intelligent, armoured, and unquestioningly obedient! When I lead them to attack Bellus, your kinsmen will find out just how superior I have always been. Just like those unfortunate Bellori patrols did.'

'All your Meta-Karith *and* Nara-Karith against a few outnumbered Bellori patrols?' Keller said. 'Is that your idea of a fair fight?'

'Don't get sentimental,' said Sudor. 'Those hapless Bellori fools were nothing more than resources for my army. Their armour, I reforge in the workshop to fit my creatures. Their weapons and ships, I put to good use. Slaying my enemies with their own weapons . . . I think that has a certain poetic justice, don't you?'

Ayl huddled on the floor, hoping Sudor would think he was cowering in fear.

He focused his mind on Sudor's, desperately trying to break through. If he could dominate the huge Bellori's consciousness for even a few moments, he might be able to buy the others enough time to get out of here alive. It might mean his own death – but he was willing to take the risk.

His mental assault crumbled at the first attempt. Sudor's mind was like a fortress. Layer upon layer of sheer, obstinate willpower surrounded it.

In its very centre he could sense Sudor's own image of himself, a giant god-like figure made from fire and destruction. No wonder the tyrant spoke of himself as superior. He truly believed he was.

If Sudor had felt Ayl's mental probing, he did not show it. Ayl gathered his strength and tried another assault, focusing all of his mind power in one area, trying to find a weak spot. His memories, perhaps . . .

It was no good. He might as well be shouting against the thunder. Sudor came stomping across the floor towards him and Ayl cowered back in genuine fear. But no – he was just coming to gloat at Dray some more. He hadn't even registered Ayl's efforts.

In desperation, not knowing what else he could do, Ayl reached out to the one mind he knew would always hear him, no matter how far from home he was.

Mother?

Faintly, across the unimaginable spaces between the stars, her answer came.

Here, my son.

Ayl sent her a mental image of what was happening to them. *He's too strong! What am I supposed to do?*

Her answer baffled him. *There is strength in unity. Didn't I tell you so back on Cantor? Do not seek to stand alone, Ayl. Become a part of something greater than yourself.*

Ayl stared at Sudor, wondering what his mother could possibly have meant. Then he saw something that made his eyes widen. On the deep space scanner behind Sudor, a large blip had become visible.

Ayl saw the tracery of glowing letters forming beneath it: *BELLORI FLAGSHIP ASTYANAX, THREAT LEVEL ULTRAVIOLET.* Warning lights were flashing madly, but silently.

Ayl glanced quickly at the control panel on Sudor's wrist. The Bellori were coming. And Sudor didn't know!

Mentally he reached out to Dray and Keller. *Don't look now,* he whispered into their minds, *but the Bellori flagship is closing in on Zarix. Whatever you do, keep him talking. We've got to make sure he doesn't notice that screen!*

Got it, Keller thought back to him. Dray sent him a mental image of her thumb sticking up.

'There's one thing I don't understand,' Keller told Sudor carefully, trading glances with Ayl. 'You said you were planning to attack Bellus first with all these Meta-Karith of yours? So what in heck were you doing on Cantor?'

'Every great army needs supplies,' Sudor explained. 'In time, I intend to strip Cantor of all its resources, leaving the Trinity System dependent on us for their food. My Meta-Karith have big appetites.'

'You want supplies?' Keller laughed. 'Then why didn't you just say? I'm sure we could work something out.'

Dray looked murderously at him, as if she would happily have broken his neck where he stood. 'Cantorians!' she said in contempt. 'Never think about anything but profit, do you?'

Ayl didn't need to look into his friends' minds to know they were putting on a convincing double act. Sudor was watching, amused, just as he was supposed to. The blip on the scanner was growing larger by the second.

'Why waste troops on a pointless invasion?' Keller said. 'There's really no need to invade us. We'd be happy

190

to sell you whatever supplies you need, at a very reasonable rate—'

'Enough!' Sudor shouted. Keller fell silent.

Did Sudor suspect? Ayl tried to see into his mind, but saw only darkness.

Dray stood facing Sudor, remembering the last time she'd squared off against the bigger, older Bellori male. That time had not ended well . . . for him.

'Your plan is pathetic,' she said slowly and deliberately. 'You're no "avenging flame of fate". You're a pitiful exile on a lonely rock, with a handful of mutant bugs for company.'

'This lonely rock is the grave of many Bellori,' Sudor replied. 'Don't worry. You'll soon be joining them.'

'You're a traitor,' she said, curling her tongue around the word. 'The Bellori army will crush your bugs underfoot, and then they will crush you.'

Inside, she was trembling. Not for fear for herself, but for her father's flagship, the *Astyanax*. They were almost in range, and if Sudor noticed, he'd trigger the ground defences. She had to keep him talking.

'You do know what will happen to you, don't you, Dray?' Sudor said matter-of-factly. 'You'll be killed by firing squad, without honour. Then, once they've gone through the motions of mourning you, you'll be forgotten about. You've always been a disappointment to your father, did you know that? Now he'll be able to wash his hands of you. Maybe he'll adopt a good strong son instead.'

Dray laughed. 'I should have killed you when I had the chance!'

Sudor slapped her then. His hand smacked her face so hard it whipped around to her shoulder.

The pain was galling. It brought water into her eyes.

Before she could move, he grabbed her hair in one hand and drew a knife with the other. His grip was tight, painful.

He jerked her head back and held the knife point to her neck. She felt the sharp sting of it. He pressed, a single hot jab. A trickle of blood steadily crawled down into the hollow at the base of her neck.

'Not so tough without your armour, are you?' His voice, close and lethal. 'Ready to die?'

Just a little longer, she thought, eyeing the screen.

'What are you looking at?' Sudor demanded, suddenly suspicious.

'Thinking about your boot-ugly face inside that helmet,' Dray said. 'I'm looking forward to putting a bullet through it.'

He put the knife point to her ear. 'I'm going to slit your throat and string you up like a slaughtered scumhog,' he snarled.

The terminal erupted with sound and light. A warning siren blared, the sound rising and falling like the screech of something alien and fighting mad. Over it all, a robotic voice was speaking. 'Bellori battle cruiser now in range. Bellori battle cruiser now in range.'

When Sudor had accused Dray of being an embarrassment to her father, the words had burned in the pit of her stomach. Even so, she'd never been so happy to see her father.

Sudor span around to face the terminals. Like the klaxon, his voice rose to a scream.

'What? A ship?' He gestured at the image on the terminal. '*What is this?*'

'My father,' said Dray. 'And your death.'

16

Sudor flung Dray away from him. Ayl caught her as she staggered.

'Get to the ships!' Sudor yelled into his wrist-com. 'Load up on grenades, frag-mines and plasma cutters!'

On the monitors they saw Nara-Karith and Meta-Karith come teeming out of the interior doors, clutching crates and bundles. The barracks was suddenly like a termite mound that had had boiling water poured into it as they scurried everywhere. Mandibles clicking, they hurried out of the main doors, heading for the ships.

'You only ambushed three patrols, didn't you?' Dray said. 'That means you only have three ships, maximum, now that your freighter's smashed to pieces. That's not nearly enough to take on a Bellori battle cruiser. Our flagship will paste you across the sky.'

'With my Meta-Karith on my side, I only need one ship,' Sudor gloated. 'Enough of this. I'm sick of the sound of your voice.' He pointed at three ordinary

Nara-Karith armed with k-guns and beckoned them over. They were silent for a moment, then nodded.

Ayl sent Dray a thought: *He's giving them orders telepathically!*

What's he saying? she thought back to him.

Ayl's thoughts were tinged with dread. '*Take these prisoners down to the processing level. Execute them.*'

The foremost Nara-Karith angled its head and made a chittering noise, as if asking a question. Sudor looked angry, but said nothing.

It's confused, Ayl explained to Dray. *It wants to be told how to kill us, what to do with our bodies . . . he's having to explain everything.*

One of the Nara-Karith gripped Ayl's upper arm hard enough to hurt. It half-led, half-dragged him down the access ramp towards a dreary concrete staircase at the back of the complex. Behind him, Dray and Keller were being hauled along, too.

Sudor waved as the heavy doors to the command dome began to slide shut. 'Goodbye, children. We won't meet again. I'll be sure to tell your parents what happened to you.'

The Nara-Karith marched them down the stairs and through a short red-lit corridor. Through large windows they saw into a room that must once have been a weapons range, but was now a workshop and storeroom.

'Look,' Dray said in a choked voice. Tables had been arranged in rows and on each one was a dead Bellori warrior. Nara-Karith stood hunched over the tables, using laser-cutters to slice the Bellori armour off in pieces.

Ayl averted his eyes, rather than watch the Nara-Karith defile the dead.

'At least they won't get *my* armour,' Dray said bitterly as they walked. 'My father will tear Sudor's head off when he finds out what he's done! He'll avenge me . . . won't he?' she asked, her voice cracking.

'Of course he will,' Ayl reassured his friend. 'But we're not going to die.'

Ayl wished he actually believed what he was telling Dray.

They entered an area of sterile metal corridors and storage bunkers. The Nara-Karith marched them through the twisting maze until they finally reached a featureless room that smelled of chemical fuel. At the far end, Ayl saw a barred metal door with a warning symbol on it: a flame in a circle. The incinerator.

'End of the line,' Keller said with black humour. 'Everybody out.'

Nobody laughed.

As the Nara-Karith moved them into position up against the wall, Ayl tried to override Sudor's orders with commands of his own. But Sudor was too close, his will too strong to breach. Instead, Ayl reached out with his mind to his friends. Urgent thoughts passed from his brain to theirs:

I'm going to try something, but I need you both to trust me. Don't say anything. Just try to relax and let me channel the power of your minds. Nod if you understand!

He watched anxiously. First Keller, then Dray gave the tiniest of nods.

OK. I need to draw on every bit of mental power you've got. Don't hold anything back. Just let go . . .

The three Nara-Karith took up their positions facing them. Ayl muttered a quick prayer as they lifted their weapons.

Keller looked at the raised gun barrels with silent defiance, looking more like a king than he ever had before. Dray was pale, trembling and tight-lipped.

The Nara-Karith aimed – and fired.

Dray was on the verge of tears as the guns fired. It wasn't the fact of her death. It was the dishonour.

On Bellus, only the lowest criminal filth – traitors

and deserters – deserved a firing squad. It was an insult as well as a punishment. It said: you deserve to be killed without a weapon in your hand. You deserve not even the slightest chance to fight back. We deny you the honour of combat.

She kept her eyes open. At least she would meet death face to face, not hiding her eyes like a blindfolded coward. She could claw back that much honour, if nothing else.

She saw the muzzles flash, heard the echoing blast.

Then her despair gave way to wonder. A bullet, rotating slowly, was hovering in mid-air in front of her chest.

It's an explosive shell, type 7, she thought crazily. She could see the little markings on it, the rifling scratches, the crimson tip. *Am I dreaming?*

The bullets aimed at Keller and Ayl were frozen in mid-air too. Ayl was staring like a madman, trembling all over, the veins standing out on his smooth forehead. Dray's mouth widened in an O of understanding.

Telekinesis! Like in the factory!

She drew a breath to speak, but never got the chance. Ayl hadn't finished. He gave a groan of effort that became a roar that became an agonized shriek.

The bullets abruptly shot back the way they had

198

come. Toward the three startled Nara-Karith who had fired them.

Three shattering explosions shook the room, repainting the dull grey walls in hues of ochre and bright yellow. Something wet flew past Dray's face and slammed into the wall behind her. When she looked again, there was no trace of the three aliens, just a mess like bugs squashed on a hover-bike's windshield.

Ayl blinked once, said, 'Excellent,' in a clear calm voice, and promptly fell over.

Dray caught him before his head hit the plascrete floor. 'Way to go, Blue!' she murmured affectionately. 'Way to go.'

'He's passed out,' Keller said. 'Dray—'

The Bellori girl was holding Ayl's limp body in her arms. 'He saved us, Keller. *Again.*'

A trickle of blood was running from Ayl's nose.

'He keeps pushing himself harder and harder,' Keller said. 'You don't think—'

'Don't say it! I'm taking him to a medical bay!' Dray said fiercely. 'There's got to be one in here!'

'Can you carry him?'

'All the way to Aquanthis if I have to.'

Ayl opened his eyes and peered up at her, groggy and unfocused. 'Are we going for a swim?'

'We will, one day,' Keller grinned. 'Just not right now. Welcome back.'

'Can you walk?' Dray said, lowering Ayl to his feet.

Ayl stood, a little shakily. He tried a couple of steps. 'Yeah. I'll be all right.' He wiped his bloodied nose. 'Killer headache, but my legs still work.'

'Good. We're still alive. Let's keep it that way.' Dray grabbed the guns dropped by the Nara-Karith and tossed one to each of her friends.

She chambered a new round with a clunk-click. 'Ready? Let's go!'

Dray moved stealthily back down the corridors, signalling to the others that the way ahead was clear. The corridors had been empty of Nara-Karith so far. Dray guessed they had all gone to board the stolen Bellori ships.

At first she'd been worried that someone would come to investigate the gunshots and find the remains of the dead aliens, but then she realized she was being stupid. Sudor had told those Nara-Karith to execute the three of them. The gunshots made it sound like the job had been done.

They drew up level with the windows that looked in on the workshop they passed earlier. Dray drew a sharp breath. There were still Nara-Karith in there, slicing the armour off the dead Bellori.

'That one,' Dray said, pointing to a bearded corpse. 'I know him. That's Colonel Ruskot, one of my father's commanders. The closest thing he had to a friend . . .'

Keller put a comforting hand on her shoulder. She didn't flinch.

'We can't let them do this,' she said. 'Come on.'

'Right behind you,' he promised.

They burst into the room. Before the Nara-Karith could react, Dray and Keller opened up with the k-guns.

Dray felt a savage joy as she blasted one after the other, blowing them away where they stood. The cutting tools they had been using went flying.

'No more butcher's work for you!' she said, blasting a Nara-Karith full in the chest. Yellow blood sprayed everywhere as it fell, thrashing, to the floor.

Dray fired and fired again without saying another word, efficient as a killing machine, pausing only to reload. Every single shot was on the mark. In less than a minute, they were the only living things in the room. More than a dozen Nara-Karith lay dead, some still twitching from muscular reflex.

'So, what now?' Keller asked. 'We can't just blast our way out topside. Ayl, can you screen us again?'

Ayl rubbed his forehead. 'I'm sorry, guys. I haven't

got my strength back. Maybe if we rest here for a while . . .'

Dray was looking at the scavenged Bellori armour, heaped up against the wall. 'No. I've got a better idea. The Nara-Karith were taking prisoners, remember? So let's find them and join forces! They have to be here somewhere!'

Keller chuckled. 'Good plan. This armour will fit them better than the bugs!'

'Cracking jokes?' Dray said angrily. 'At a time like this?'

'I was just trying to, you know, lighten the mood . . .' His voice faltered.

'Have some respect,' she told him, closing Colonel Ruskot's eyes. 'For the dead, at least, if you can't have any for yourself.'

'Don't you two start arguing again,' Ayl warned. 'My head's aching enough as it is. Come on.'

Dray led the search through the barracks, down gloomy vacant corridors and past empty rooms that had once been billets but were now nests for the Nara-Karith. The acrid stench of the creatures was everywhere, but there were none to be found.

Turning a corner, she froze as she saw the humped shape of a Meta-Karith ahead. When it didn't attack, she advanced carefully. It was only a skin, empty and brittle.

'They must shed their skins as they grow,' Ayl mused. 'Makes sense. They grow pretty big . . .'

'Hey!' called a gruff voice from behind a heavy door. 'Who's out there?'

'This is Dray, daughter of General Iccus. We're here to bust you out!'

Dray shot at the lock with her k-gun and Keller kicked the door in. Lieutenant Rokar and the twelve surviving Bellori he commanded wasted no time with pleasantries, quickly filling the trio in on all they knew as they headed up to the arsenal. Sudor, they learned, had one more ship than expected; his personal warship, a top-of-the-range Bellori Deathblade, was in a landing bay outside.

'The customized ship we found on Cantor must be the one he escaped from Bellus in,' Keller said. 'I don't understand where he got a brand new Deathblade from, though.'

'I do,' Lieutenant Rokar said. 'Sudor used to command hundreds of ships. It must be part of his old fleet, hidden away in secret. He probably changed the records to make it look like it was destroyed.'

'We need to get out of here,' Keller urged. 'Question is, what do we do next? Help the Bellori troops fight back?'

'We go straight to Sudor and kill him, of course!' Dray said.

'No,' Rokar said firmly. 'He is sealed in the command dome, beyond our reach for now. Dray is our priority. She must be taken to her father on his flagship.'

'I'm not a child!' Dray bristled. 'I don't need to be protected!'

'With respect, you are the heir to the command of Bellus. We must get you to safety. With all the stolen Firehawks launched already, there is only one way to do this.'

'Steal Sudor's Deathblade?' said Ayl.

'Exactly. I'm certain it is still here, prepared for launch.'

'Sudor would never leave himself without an escape route,' Dray agreed. 'Very well. Lead the way, Lieutenant.'

As they made their way back to the surface, Keller was almost disappointed there were no Nara-Karith in the corridors. Rokar and his comrades would have shot them to pieces.

Almost at the exit, Keller looked up as they passed beneath the command dome.

As they walked, Dray muttered to him, 'Sudor's in there. We could kill him now and put an end to all this. But no, loyal Rokar has to haul me back to my father like a lost family pet.'

The landing bay was nothing more than a flat plascrete platform round the back of the barracks, with bright orange luxoglobes marking the individual landing points. Sudor's ship was at the far side, a sleek black and red craft like an Inui Shadowfalcon with its wings folded.

'There's the Deathblade,' Keller said. 'Looks clear. We should make a dash for— Ayl!' The Aquanth was clutching his head again. 'What's wrong?'

'Meta-Karith!' Ayl said, pointing. Two of the gigantic insectile beasts were clambering out of the ship and heading towards them. 'I could hear their thoughts. Sudor's elite guard!'

Keller swore.

Rokar and his men took aim with their rifles. 'We'll keep them occupied, Dray. You three need to get aboard that ship!'

Keller hesitated. 'You're not coming with us? But – those things will *kill* you!'

The Meta-Karith were charging now, their limbs tearing at the concrete.

'It was a shameful thing to be defeated and taken prisoner,' Rokar growled, sighting down the length of his rifle. 'We shall stand and fight, and regain our honour. Tell General Iccus we did our duty.'

'Lieutenant—'

'Run! NOW!'

Keller grabbed Dray and ran, followed close behind by Ayl. The Meta-Karith came lurching after them.

The landing bay lit up like the heart of a fusion reactor as the Bellori opened fire. Bursts of pulse rifle fire hammered the Meta-Karith, sending them staggering. Most of the shots pummelled their thick armour, but some struck them in their limbs, sending yellow gore spraying.

Leaving a trail of blood and body parts in their wake, the Meta-Karith changed course and bore down on the soldiers. Keller knew what would happen next. He didn't want to see them die, however bravely.

Dray dived inside the ship, closely followed by Ayl. As Keller passed through the hatch, he quickly slammed the emergency lock control. The doors hissed and began to close.

A clawed limb shot up through the hatchway and

slashed at Keller's arm.

There was another one of those kracking things under the ship, he realized desperately. *I'm dead.*

Like steel shears, the Meta-Karith's arm sliced at Keller, cutting through the sleeve of his jumpsuit but narrowly missing his arm. Expecting to hear the bone in his arm snap, Keller heard another sound – the deep crunch of the closing doors biting through the Meta-Karith's limb.

The doors wheezed, then slammed shut with a final clang. The arm fell to the floor, severed, but still blindly trying to grasp. It brushed Keller's foot.

Keller didn't have time to be sickened. He kicked it away and joined the others on the ship's command deck, rubbing his throbbing arm.

Now *this* was a ship to be reckoned with – a brand new Bellori assault craft, fast and manoeuvrable.

'Strap yourselves in,' he said, taking the helm. 'This is where the fun starts.'

17

Ayl gripped the arms of his seat.

Flying again. He'd never get used to it. And now, Sudor's army was trying to kill him.

'Need to fire up the engines,' Keller observed. 'Dray? Where the heck do you people keep the power control console?'

'On a Deathblade? It's over there,' she pointed. 'Targeting and gunnery there, nav there, shields and repair systems there . . . don't look at me like that, Keller!'

'You're kidding me! How many people are *meant* to fly this thing?'

'Ten Bellori officers,' she admitted. 'With academy training.'

'We're going to improvize,' Keller said, cracking his knuckles. 'Ayl, get to the power controls and start this baby up. Dray, you're on shields and repair. Everything else we'll just have to make up as we go along!'

Reluctantly, Ayl moved to his control panel. An image of the ship glowed there, with its power distribution flow marked out in pulsing lines. He had no idea what any of it meant. His head was still throbbing.

'Ayl?' barked Keller. 'Are you with us?'

'Sorry!' Ayl said. 'That mind control stunt with the bullets took a lot out of me. My brain's pretty fried. I can barely think straight.'

Ayl had never flown a ship before in his life. *It can't be too hard*, he thought. *Just got to stay calm*. He clicked on a likely-looking button, and was rewarded with the rumble of mighty fusion turbines powering up.

'Nice work!' Keller yelled.

With a thunderous boom of igniting engines, they took off.

The ship rocked from one side to the other as Keller tried out some moves. Ayl blew out his cheeks and tried to focus on his screen. *So far so good*, he told himself.

'We've got multiple inbound ships on the targeting scope!' Dray yelled from the main gunnery console.

'What? I thought I told you to get to shields and repair, not weapons!' Keller said, exasperated.

'If you're half the pilot I think you are, we won't need

the repair systems,' she snapped. 'You do your job, and let me do mine.'

'Inbound *hostile* ships?' Ayl asked cautiously.

'No way to tell. Our flagship has an escort of twelve Firehawks, the same model as Sudor captured.'

'Oh, krack,' Keller swore. 'Can you contact your father over the coms system?'

'Coms is that one there. You want me to change consoles? We'll be in weapon range in thirty clicks and counting.'

'OK. OK. Going to head for the flagship and hope any ships we see near it are your people, not Sudor's. Blue, take the hyperdrive offline and patch the spare power through to the shields!'

Ayl struggled to work out how he was meant to do that. He flipped through screenfuls of schematics. Intricate power flows unfolded before him. They just looked like tangled shara-weeds.

Something nagged at his mind. He realized Dray was trying to send him a mental image. A spiky golden ball, rotating, with lines coming off it.

Hyperdrive icon, she thought to him.

Suddenly aware of what he was looking for, he found the right sequence of controls and tapped them in. The golden ball darkened on the screen and several bars of energy on the right filled up with fresh bright colour.

'Shields at maximum!' he called out. He sent a thought to Dray: *You're becoming quite the telepath!*

'All right!' said Keller. 'Let's go say hello to Dray's family. And there they are!'

The *Astyanax* hung in space like a broad, flat spearhead levelled at Zarix. Ayl couldn't tell if the three Bellori Firehawks heading for it were closing in for the attack or moving to protect it.

'We mustn't fire on any of those ships!' Dray warned. 'We need to know they're definitely hostile before we fire a single shot!'

One of the ships broke formation and headed towards them.

Ayl stared. 'They're checking us out.'

'Let them get close,' Dray said evenly. 'I'm pretty sure it's one of ours.'

'They aren't acting hostile,' Keller agreed. 'Staying on course.'

Ayl squinted at the approaching ship, identical to their own. He was too exhausted for telepathy, but forced himself to open his mind. Just in case.

Destroy, rasped the Nara-Karith voices in his head. *Destroy. Destroy.*

Ayl sat bolt upright in his chair. 'Keller! They're firing! SWERVE!'

Keller banked hard as the ship came swooping down towards them. A tracery of mass driver fire ripped through the air.

'Are we hit?' Keller yelled.

Ayl scrambled over to the shields and repair console. 'No. Shields took a pounding but we're OK!'

Keller pulled the ship around in a wide, screaming arc, as Dray fired bursts from the wing cannon, hitting nothing but empty space.

'Come on, bugs!' he grunted. 'Where the hell are you?'

Dray's console began to make a shrill, beeping noise. Her face filled with horror. 'Keller, they've got a missile lock on us! Going to try to jam . . .'

'They're on our tail!' Ayl shouted. 'Giving you all the spare power we've got! Can you lose them?'

Keller threw the ship into a veering loop. 'Doing my best!'

The bleeping from Dray's console turned to a constant whine.

'Tracking missile fired!' Dray howled. 'Red trace . . . it's a mini-nuke!'

'Hang on!' Keller banked as the whine grew louder.

Ayl closed his eyes and prayed.

* * *

'Still locked on. Impact in five,' Dray said.

As the Bellori counted down the few remaining clicks she had left to live, Keller felt the world around him slow down to a strange timeless drift.

He suddenly saw himself as a child, running across the palace lawns after his father, laughing. Then he was in the Fire Cellar with his friends, whooping it up after buying a caseload of zentimah pearls for a pittance.

'Four,' said Dray.

He was in the Mazakomi, soaring through the finishing laser-grid in first place . . . Dancing under the twin moons of Lustria . . . Walking through the palace gardens with King Lial.

You really do see your life flash before you, thought Keller. *I'm going to die.*

It had been a full life. A crazy, exciting, good life. But now it was ending, before he'd ever worn the Crown of Cantor.

Faces flashed before him. Tyrus, bellowing. The girl with the blistered mouth. The trembling slave on the block. The overseer. The cadaverous-faced man.

Things that needed putting right.

'Three,' said Dray, her voice dead.

Damn it, I'm not ready to die yet. There's stuff I still need to do.

Keller hit the afterburners and powered the Deathblade into a crash dive.

The missile swooped to follow them, zeroing in on the blazing engines at their rear. The micro-nuke warhead was enough to take out a small city. It could easily obliterate a single ship.

A miscalculation now would kill them all. But if he did nothing they were dead anyway.

Keller pulled out of the dive, levelled off and went roaring over the moon's surface a mere few paces above it. The pursuing missile adjusted its course an instant too late and slammed into the ground.

A sphere of pure white light expanded behind them, followed immediately by a wave of indescribable noise. The explosion threw up a tsunami of dirt and rock. A vast shockwave buffeted the craft, but Keller was already pulling back up and gaining height.

'Still alive,' he gasped. 'That. Was. Close.'

Dray laughed in sheer disbelieving delight. 'You're amazing!'

'*We're* amazing,' Keller corrected her. 'Nicely done, people.'

Keller brought them back up to the high outer edge of the atmosphere where the Bellori craft were dogfighting.

'Oh, hell,' he said, crestfallen. The triumph of a few moments ago evaporated in an instant. 'Look at the monitors!'

Meta-Karith were clambering out of open hatchways on Sudor's ships and launching themselves at the Bellori craft. They fired hissing jets of vapour from crevices in their bodies, using them to steer themselves through space.

Keller watched in horror as one of the monsters soared all the way on to the outer hull of a Bellori ship, clung and held on. It clamped a bulky metal disc there and scuttled back.

'It's a frag mine!' Dray said. 'They're *boarding*!'

The mine detonated, ripping a whole section of the hull away. A helpless Bellori warrior floated off into the vacuum from inside the ship, struggling desperately. The Meta-Karith climbed inside like a rotwasp writhing into a decayed samthorn fruit.

'There's another!' Ayl said, pointing out another Bellori Firehawk.

Two Meta-Karith had already latched on and were deploying their mines. The ship veered and rocked as the pilot tried to shake them off, but the creatures' grip was unbreakable.

'Let's help the Bellori out,' Keller said, bringing their own ship around in pursuit. 'Dray, pick a target and lock on!'

'On it!'

Keller moved in behind the other Bellori ship, hoping the crew wouldn't think he was attacking *them*. The Meta-Karith were moving in with frightening speed.

'Locked on,' Dray said. 'Firing!'

A hot streak of exhaust cut across their view. The missile struck one of the creatures, which became an expanding fireball.

Dray whooped. 'One down! Wait. Lost the signal. Where's the other one?'

With a thud, something struck their own hull.

Keller knew what had happened even before he saw the creature scrabbling across the hull. The Meta-Karith had changed targets.

Now it was going to board *them*.

Dray struggled to lock the ship's guns on the creature. Keller kept yelling, 'Bug on the ship!' – as if it wasn't obvious.

'We've got problems!' Ayl said ominously. 'Another ship inbound and closing fast.'

'Thanks for the warning!' Keller grated, swerving out of the incoming ship's line of fire just in time. It roared past above them.

'They're coming round for another pass,' Ayl warned.

Dray ground her teeth in frustration. Every time she came close to getting a target lock, Keller had to swing the ship out of the way of a flurry of enemy fire and she lost her aim.

'Bug's got his frag mine ready,' Keller said. 'Don't want to worry you guys, but if he blows the hull open, we'll all be eating vacuum.'

Dray's console began to make the shrill beeping noise again. 'Oh, krack,' she swore, looking at the red blip moving toward their craft. 'That other ship's locked on and firing!' *We're right back where we were*, she thought, *except with a bug on our windscreen*. 'Twenty clicks till impact.'

'Taking evasive action!' Keller yelled.

As he tried to shake the missile off, a dull clunk echoed through the ship. The Meta-Karith had clamped the mine in place.

'OK!' Dray yelled, taking charge. 'Everyone to the life pod!'

'What?' Keller said, bewildered.

'No time to argue. We have to bail out.'

Her decision burned in her gut. It felt so much like cowardice, like running away.

But this wasn't a battle they could win and she knew it. With a missile bearing down on them and a mine about to blow their hull open, the ship was as good as destroyed.

'Suit up, quick, and make sure you're holding on to something!' she said, pulling Ayl and Keller out of their seats and over to the circular hole in the floor that was the emergency exit shaft. They pulled the silver suits on over their clothes, fastening their helmets in place as fast as they could manage.

The beeping turned into a constant screech.

Dray locked her helmet seal, muffling the noise, and shoved Keller down the laddered chute into the escape pod. Ayl jumped down after him. Just as Dray grabbed the topmost rung, an explosion ripped through the front of the ship.

The cockpit's contents flew out in a storming gale, loose handguns, papers and grenades whirling into the empty void. Now hurricane winds were dragging at Dray, threatening to tear her out of the ship. Oblivious to the winds of decompression, the Meta-Karith was climbing in. It was on the ceiling.

Without Keller at the helm, the ship spun wildly out of control. There was no longer any up or down. Dray hung on to the ladder bars, winds whistling round her, climbing hand over hand toward the pod. Keller reached out a hand to her and pulled her the rest of the way into the tiny, cramped space.

Dray kicked the illuminated button that read LAUNCH. The iris valve closed with a sharp hiss.

'Hold on to your seats,' she said grimly. 'We're getting out of here!'

18

In the soundless vacuum of space, the three friends couldn't hear the separation charges detonate. They felt their effect, however, as they were flung against the pod's padded interior.

The stars wheeled madly around them as the spinning pod shot into space, rocketing away from the doomed ship like a ball fired from a cannon.

Floating together, bereft of gravity, the three of them watched the Deathblade explode in the distance. First the main drive blew up in a blaze of white light, then all the warheads in the arsenal exploded in fireballs of orange and scarlet. It would have been beautiful if it hadn't been such a disaster.

'That could have gone better,' Keller said blandly. 'At least we're alive, eh?'

He felt cold and dead inside, though. To have escaped from so much already, just to end up here! Out of the frying pan, and into the endless freezing void of space. At least fire would have been warm, he thought ruefully.

He could joke all he liked but he was still stuck here, trapped in a lifepod with battle raging in the distance and no way to help. Through the fabric of his spacesuit he felt his father's ring on his finger, twisting it like a lucky charm. What would Trade King Lial have done in a situation like this?

No. That line of thinking would lead nowhere. Trade King Lial was dead, and all the wishing in the world wouldn't bring him back. The question was: What was Trade King Keller going to do?

If I'd wanted to be stuck with these guys miles from anywhere, I might as well have stayed on Cantor, he thought to himself. *At least the safe house would have had the basics, like food and drink, furniture, and all the air I could breathe.*

'We're losing ships,' Dray said hollowly. The distant flashes and explosions were reflected in her helmet visor. 'Sudor's pets are tearing the Bellori fleet apart.'

'So what do we do?' Ayl said.

'What *can* we do?' said Dray, turning away from the battle. 'My people are getting ripped to pieces out there! We've got far more ships than Sudor does, but just one of those Meta-Karith can rip its way in through the hull. We've got more warriors, but what good is a Bellori warrior if he's floating in space without a suit?'

'We can't give up, Dray,' Keller said. 'Not now.'

'Face facts! The Meta-Karith are just too strong! I hate him, but Sudor was right. They're just like Bellori, only better!'

'You want facts?' Keller said harshly. 'Then get comfortable, because I'm going to give you some facts! Fact one: those things are stronger, but we're smarter. Seriously, they are *dumb as krack*.'

'Hey, you're right,' Ayl said excitedly. 'They're like machines, just following orders! That's what their minds feel like from the inside.'

Keller took a breath. 'Fact two: we're fighting for a cause we believe in. That means we don't give up. We don't ask the odds. And we do whatever it takes to get the job done, even if it means doing something crazy.'

'Where are you going with this, Keller?' Dray asked suspiciously.

'Answer me this. Who are the best warriors in the galaxy?'

'The Bellori, of course,' Dray said.

'So if you want to beat the best, you need to build a better Bellori warrior?' Keller asked.

'Why are you even asking?' Dray snapped. 'You know that's what Sudor's done!'

'And you're still thinking like him, and that's why you're losing!' Keller insisted. 'If Sudor's army are beating your people at their own game, then it's time to change the game.'

Dray stared at him.

'The Bellori are the underdogs this time!' Keller went on, hoping Dray wasn't about to punch straight through his visor. 'You've been on top for so long, you've forgotten what that's like. You've never had to adapt. Am I right?'

Dray stared at him.

'Sudor's based his whole strategy on doing what the Bellori do, only doing it better. So the only way for you to win is to stop acting like Bellori!'

Dray stared at him. It was becoming unnerving.

'Dray?'

'We need to speak to my father,' she said. 'Right now.'

'Erm . . . small problem there, Dray,' said Keller. 'Life-pods aren't steerable. They lock on to the nearest habitable world and head for it. Because the occupants are often unconscious after an accident or battle—'

'I do know that!' she interrupted. 'Can't you make this thing move with your thoughts, Ayl?'

'It's a bit bigger than a bullet,' Ayl pondered. Seeing Dray's face, he added, 'But I'll try.'

Why shouldn't I be able to move it? he reasoned. *I've surprised myself a lot today.*

He closed his eyes and tried to feel the outline of the lifepod with his mind. It was coasting through space, needing only a subtle push to change its course. He focused his mind and *willed* the lifepod to change direction.

He might as well have been trying to move a boulder by blowing on it. He was still exhausted from saving their lives in the barracks. If he'd had more strength left . . . He groaned in frustration.

'Come on, Blue!' Dray urged.

Ayl didn't want to let Dray down. He exerted himself in a last, final push . . . and let go, gasping.

'We've changed course,' Keller announced, studying a panel. 'By . . . let's see . . . a fraction of a degree. Not nearly enough, I'm afraid.'

'I'm sorry.' Ayl panted. 'It's just too big for me to move on my own. Even the three of us together won't be able to move it.'

'You did move it,' Keller said encouragingly.

'Yeah, by a hair's breadth!' Dray said, clearly frustrated. 'This is hopeless. We're stuck.'

'No, guys, we can do this!' Keller unfastened an emergency window breaker and began to prise the top off the control panel with it. With a crackle and a fizz, the screen went black and the lights died.

'Um. I really don't want to be negative or anything, but I think you just fried the lifepod computer,' Ayl said.

'Yep,' said Keller. 'That's the idea.'

'Uh, Keller?' Ayl said in a worried voice. 'Did you hit your head on the way in?'

Keller had the console open now and was tinkering with the wires inside. 'The computer's programmed to take us to the nearest planet,' he said. 'But we don't want to go there, we want to go in the other direction. So we bypass the computer.'

'You're hotwiring the lifepod engines!' Dray said in disbelief.

Keller grinned back at her, pressed a few controls, and sat back in satisfaction as the lights came back on.

Ayl felt himself drift back against the wall. 'We're moving!' he said. 'You did it!'

'I did say it was a *small* problem,' Keller said. 'Now,

225

if you'll excuse me, I still have to steer this thing . . .'

Steering, Ayl noted, turned out to mean brushing bare wires together to fire the port or starboard manoeuvring jets. Keller swore a lot, but Ayl had to admit he knew what he was doing.

They were moving steadily towards the *Astyanax* now. To Ayl's relief, it looked undamaged. For now.

A Firehawk swept past near them, with Meta-Karith flinging themselves out of the hatches. One of Sudor's, clearly. Ayl held his breath, waiting for the sickening thump of one of them landing on the hull. It never came.

'I guess a lifepod is too small for them to bother with,' Dray said, echoing his own thoughts.

Ayl braced himself for the fighting he knew would come. Once the Bellori fighter craft were down, the hybrids would turn their attention to the flagship. Even if their lifepod was taken on board the *Astyanax*, there was no safe haven there. The violence and bloodshed were far from over.

The huge airlock closed its jaws beneath the pod, sealing the flagship's hangar off from the hunger of space. As gravity was steadily restored, the pod settled on the hangar floor.

'Atmosphere initiation complete,' rang a voice over the ship's public address system. 'Exit at will.'

Dray popped the hatch and clambered out on to the flight deck. Knowing the iron might of the Bellori flagship was all around her was thrilling. Many times today, she had come within inches of death. Now she felt empowered, back in her domain.

She checked herself. She had to remember that Sudor had the advantage. Keller had been right. She couldn't fall back into the old Bellori ways and expect to win.

General Iccus, flanked by two attendants, came hurrying across to her. 'Dray?' he said, his voice registering bewilderment and relief at once. 'When I gave the command to investigate Zarix, I never dreamed you would be here!' He stopped in his tracks, realising what he was seeing. 'Where is your armour?'

'On Cantor,' she said, shame stealing over her face. 'It was a necessary deception.'

'We can speak of that later. I'm glad to see you alive and standing.' He nodded at the bloodstained bandage on her arm. 'You're wounded.'

'It was the Nara-Karith, and a new giant breed of them called Meta-Karith,' she said. 'Father, I have much to tell you.'

'Accompany me to the command deck, then, and talk as we go.'

With Ayl and Keller filling in details, Dray gave her report. She carefully avoided any suggestion of heroism on her part or her friends'. Iccus listened, nodded, and took notes, as if she had been any other officer.

They arrived on the command deck, where Bellori officers were bent over terminals and studying terrain holograms.

'We have a squadron of heavy assault fighters docked and readying for launch,' he told Dray. 'No more prevarication. You've proved your worth. I'm giving you command of your own ship. Crew will be provided.'

Once, Dray would have leapt at that chance. But now she said, 'I have a better idea, father.'

Iccus loomed over her. 'You are *refusing* the honour of command?'

'Permission to speak, sir!' she demanded. 'I know how we can beat Sudor's army!'

Every Bellori general in the room turned to listen.

Iccus nodded for her to continue.

'The creatures have been ordered to attack our warriors,' Dray explained. 'They will carry out that order without deviation or question. They may be strong, but they're dumb as . . . well, they have no imagination. If they're given an order, they won't do anything except carry it out until they get given a new order, even if the situation changes. They can only have one plan at a time.'

'Sudor will surely have considered multiple strategies!' Iccus objected. 'Do not underestimate his tactical ability.'

'Sudor already thinks he is going to win,' Dray said. 'He won't have programmed his troops with a backup plan. He's too arrogant for that. And they don't have the capacity to think independently, so they won't come up with one themselves.'

'So how do you propose we thwart him?' asked Iccus, sceptical but intrigued.

Dray took a breath. It was now or never.

'We take the battle to the surface of Zarix and leave empty suits of Bellori armour as a decoy target. Sudor's using our scanners and they track armour, not the person wearing it. The empty armour will look like a real invasion force, and both the Nara-Karith and the Meta-Karith have been ordered to attack anything that looks like a Bellori soldier. We'll lure his super-warriors into a trap!'

'Far too dangerous!' Iccus said. 'Remove our armour?

The armour that has made the Bellori army the most powerful fighting force in the galaxy?'

'Yes!' Dray yelled.

'Unthinkable.'

'Yes! It's *unthinkable* that the Bellori would ever take their armour off deliberately. And that's why we have to try it – *because Sudor would never think of it either!*'

'Absurd.'

'Sudor would say the same thing! We can't fight in the old ways this time. He'll be expecting that! Father, please. This is the only way!'

Iccus shook his head. 'I admire your passion, my daughter. It is a bold plan. But it risks far too much.' He turned to walk away.

'Sir?' said Keller. 'Might I have permission to speak?'

Iccus considered, then nodded.

Keller stepped forward. 'Who is this person?' he asked, and pointed at Dray.

'My daughter, Dray,' Iccus said. 'As you know. What is your point?'

Keller shook his head. 'No, sir. This is a trained Bellori warrior. More than that – she's an expert military tactician. She studied at the best military academy and has proven her skill in combat. Even at her young age, she is the equal of anyone in this room.'

'I fail to see—'

'With respect, sir, that's exactly the problem,' Keller said. 'You *fail to see* the military genius standing in front of you. You only see your daughter.'

Keller took another step forward. 'This is her moment, General. It's what she's trained for all her life! If you can't see her as anything other than your daughter, then you're robbing us all of the one person who knows how to beat Sudor, the one person who ever *has* beaten him!'

Keller was nearly shouting now. 'You know what that means. The whole Trinity System will fall before him. And you will be responsible for that, General.'

19

Ayl could sense the volcanic emotion trapped inside General Iccus's armour. It was about to explode, and Keller was the target. For a moment it seemed Ayl might need to step in.

But Iccus did not roar with rage or grab Keller. He slowly turned to his generals.

'Order the crews to retreat,' he said. He nodded at Dray. 'You all heard the plan this warrior proposed. We are putting it into practice as of now.'

Dray and Keller exchanged a look, and Dray even managed a faint smile.

'Sir,' an officer said, 'to take the battle to the surface of Zarix, we will have to contend with Sudor's spaceborne forces and ground-to-air emplacements. Losses will be heavy.'

Iccus nodded. 'Remain out of their range for now. Plot a course that will bring the most troops to the surface alive.' He paused. 'Call for volunteers. We will need some ships to sacrifice themselves by drawing enemy fire. The honour will be great.'

As the Bellori bravely carried out their orders, Ayl felt a mixture of sadness and admiration. These Bellori were preparing to make themselves vulnerable by removing their armour. Some would even lay down their lives in the next ten minutes, just to give others a chance. They were taking a terrible risk, without help from any other quarter.

He couldn't let them do this alone. He had to get help.

If the Bellori were willing to change their minds about something so fundamental, maybe the Aquanths could too. It had to be worth a try.

He reached out with his mind, bridging the distances between the stars. *Mother. I need to talk to you.*

Ayl! You are safe! He felt her joy. *When I heard you were missing—*

I'm fine, he interrupted. *There's a lot I need to tell you. So much is changing, especially in me. But first, I need you to call a conclave. The whole planet needs to hear this.*

Ayl did not know if it was down to the new authority and power he felt, or just her own belief in him, but his mother immediately did as he asked. He could feel her sending out the telepathic signal, calling all Aquanth minds together across the planet, linking them together as one.

Conclave, went the whisper from mind to mind, as Aquanth after Aquanth joined the network. *Conclave!* They were hushed, expectant. They knew nothing of what the Bellori were about to face.

In moments, the conclave was assembled. Ayl felt waves of shared emotion as he joined his own mind to the collective: revulsion, suspicion, and more than anything else, fear. All directed at him.

I bring grave news, he beamed out to them. *The Nara-Karith have returned.*

Shockwaves spread across the planet.

Speak on, his mother urged him.

Knowing he had the attention of his whole planet, Ayl chose his next words carefully. *We've got one chance to nip this invasion in the bud. The Bellori are about to enter combat with the Nara-Karith and try to finish this once and for all. And a lot of good Bellori are going to die unless WE do something about it.*

Tens of millions of Aquanth minds recoiled in horror. He could feel their thoughts condensing into a single message:

We are pacifists! We will not participate in a war!

The idea is unthinkable!

Unthinkable. Ayl had heard that word a little too recently to have any patience with it now.

You think you can just hide behind a planetary shield and wait for it all to be over? he thought. *That won't work this time. You'll participate in a war whether you want to or not, because Sudor and his Nara-Karith are coming for you next. With the Bellori out of the way, he'll ravage our world like a maddened baneshark.*

An uproar of disquiet went through the massed minds of Aquanthis. They tried to shout him down. *Liar! You are sick from what you have seen!*

My son is no liar, Lady Moa declared forcefully. *And he is not sick. We must listen.*

The other Aquanths tried to argue. *His mind harbours images of brutality, death, terrible things . . .*

TRUE things, Ayl argued, his mind a whip lashing them into guilty silence.

You can't hide from the truth, no matter how ugly it is, he told them. *Peace is not an option now. The only choice is whether we enter a war now or later.*

Confusion, fear and dread swept over the Aquanths. *We cannot fight. So how can we help the Bellori?*

Had *he* ever been that squeamish? Ayl smiled a grim smile. *I will do it for you. Lend me your mental strength and I'll do what needs to be done. Only I will carry the grisly memories.*

The Aquanths hesitated. *You would do this?*

What have I got to lose? he thought. *I'm an outcast already, aren't I?*

That set them all to murmuring.

We have always shunned conflict, his mother reminded him. *If we do this, we can never go back.*

I know, he thought. *I've crossed that blood-red river already.*

She was almost begging now: *You are asking us to break sacred tradition!*

Ayl thought of the proud Bellori who had chosen to remove their armour. *Sometimes you have to change or die. Whether it's one person or millions, the choice is the same.*

He broke the connection.

Now there was nothing to do but wait. Ayl hoped the Aquanths wouldn't take too many hours to—

We accept.

The message stunned him with its speed and simplicity.

We place the power of our thoughts under your control, the Aquanths told him. *Guide us.*

'General Iccus?' Ayl said, coming back to reality.

'I think I can get the fleet to the surface with fewer casualties.'

'Well, since I appear to be taking counsel from Cantorians now, I may as well listen to an Aquanth too. How many casualties do you expect we will sustain?'

'Erm . . . none at all.'

'Then by all means, speak!'

Moments later, with Iccus's approval, Ayl began to channel the mental power of the entire Aquanth race. He wove a cloaking field huge enough to conceal every Bellori ship, from the *Astyanax* down to the fighters.

In one instant, the Bellori vanished. Stars shone steadily through the spaces where they had been moments before.

'Sudor's ships are retreating,' an officer announced. 'They think we've jumped out of the system!'

'Good,' Iccus said. 'All ships, prepare to land on Zarix. We must remain concealed until the last possible moment. The surface of Zarix itself will be our hiding place. Conceal your ships within craters.'

The fleet descended through the stormy atmosphere, hidden behind Ayl's cloaking field. Dray pointed to the terrain display screen.

'That valley there will make a perfect killing field, Father,' she said. 'Between those two extinct volcanoes.

We can hide the ships in the craters and trap the Nara-Karith at the foot of the slopes.'

'Do as she says,' said Iccus to his crew. 'Prepare to bait the trap.'

In the narrow valley, with the grey slopes of the twin volcanoes rising to either side, Keller watched the assembled Bellori gather. Twelve hundred warriors, he thought: the combined crews of the flagship and all the surviving Firehawks. Facing off against about ten *thousand* Nara-Karith, by Iccus's estimate.

'Warriors of Bellus!' General Iccus ordered. 'Remove your armour.'

He reached up, twisted his helmet and lifted it off his head.

Suddenly, Keller was looking at a solemn, shaven-headed man of about fifty turns, with sagging jowls and grey eyes.

He has Dray's eyes, was Keller's first thought. *And he looks so very . . . ordinary.*

From all around came the sounds of catches unfastening and seams parting. Without protest, without any words spoken at all, the Bellori unceremoniously removed their armour.

Keller tried not to stare, but he couldn't help it.

Before his eyes, they changed from a horde of near-identical warrior drones to the people they had always been on the inside.

He saw men, women, young people, dark-skinned and olive-skinned, blinking in the light as if they had just emerged from a deep mine. Some looked so alike they had to be related. It had never occurred to Keller before, even despite the example of Iccus and Dray, that parents and children would serve in the army alongside one another.

In the simple, light jumpsuits they wore beneath their armour, they looked vulnerable. A stab of sympathy hit Keller under the ribs as he realized they were about to enter the most important fight of their lives, and they would be as good as naked. The only thing concealing them was Ayl's cloaking field, and even that wouldn't endure once the fighting started.

He had known Bellori were brave, but this was something new. None of them would ever have contemplated removing their armour before today, let alone fighting without it. And yet, here they were, obeying their leader without a word of objection. Because they believed what they were doing was just, and right, and necessary.

And because of General Iccus, as armourless as all

the rest, who was not asking any less of his people than he himself was willing to give.

Their bravery humbled Keller. He twisted his father's ring, thinking how much of his own authority depended upon privileges he'd never had to earn. Would his Cantorian subjects have done the same for him?

Silently, he made a vow to himself. *If I make it through this cycle alive, I swear will earn my subjects' respect. Not with pointless ceremonies, speeches and all that krack, but by standing up for what's right, like Iccus. Even if it costs me. Even if it gets me killed.*

'Arrange the suits into a standard Type 7 wedge!' Iccus commanded.

Mag-locks latched the separate armour pieces back into single suits, which could then be arrayed like mannequins. The Bellori placed their suits in a carefully posed configuration, as if they were real warriors preparing for battle.

Watching each warrior arrange his or her own suit was strange and poignant to Keller, as if the Bellori's souls had escaped and left their bodies behind.

The Bellori opened boxes of weapons and passed them around. Each one took bandoliers of grenades, hand-held rifles, swords and snub pistols. Dray looked satisfied to be reunited with proper field armament at last.

'Alpha Squadron, take position at the top of the west volcano,' Iccus ordered. 'Beta Squadron, you're in the east. Once the enemy is within range, we'll close the ends of the valley with K-grids and create a killing ground.'

The Bellori nodded, readying their weapons.

'You will all be aware that the danger, and the honour, are very great. I will therefore consider volunteers to lead the squadrons.'

Keller toyed with his father's ring one final time and clenched his hand into a fist. He stepped forward.

'General, if a Cantorian might have the honour, I would like to volunteer to lead Alpha Squadron.'

Dray's heart leapt into her mouth at Keller's request. Was he trying to make some stupid joke? Surely her father wouldn't accept!

There was a moment of silence.

'This is no ordinary battle,' Iccus said gravely. 'And you, I think, are no ordinary Cantorian. But a Bellori platoon must have a Bellori commander. Alpha Squadron, fall in under Commander Slarek. Trade King Keller will be your second-in-command.'

He raised his fist in a traditional Bellori salute. Keller returned it.

'Father, I volunteer to lead Beta Squadron!' Dray said quickly.

'Request denied.'

Dray thought for a moment that she must have misheard, but the looks on the Bellori's faces told her she had not.

She was thunderstruck. He said no.

'Request to act as second-in-command, sir.'

'Request denied.'

Damn him to hell. All he had to say was 'yes'. It would have made up for everything. Instead, he had humiliated her. Now, of all times, he was telling his people he did not accept her as a true and tested Bellori warrior.

'You trust a Cantorian more than me?' she demanded, her voice shrill with anger. 'Your own daughter?'

She shot Keller a look of bitter jealousy, but there was no ill will in the look he gave her back. He seemed older, somehow.

'It is not a matter of trust, Dray,' said Iccus. 'I cannot accept your offer to lead Beta Squadron.'

'Why?' Dray asked, struggling to keep her voice even.

'Because I have already assigned you to an even more important mission, if you are willing to accept it.'

That shocked her into near silence.

'More important than this battle?' she asked, bewildered.

'There is more than one battle to be fought today. We will attend to the main body of the enemy here,' Iccus explained. 'But *someone* must sever the head, someone whose skill in combat and infiltration is unsurpassed. If we know Sudor, he will not risk his life out here among his hybrids. He will be hiding in his bunker, commanding from a distance. He must die.'

The meaning of his words sank in.

'You want me to kill Sudor,' Dray said.

Iccus nodded.

Dray walked to the weapons crates as if she were walking on air. She put all her bulky weapons back in. None of them were appropriate to an assassination mission. She would need to be stealthy for this.

She selected only a k-gun and a short sword. That would be enough. Lastly, one of her father's aides passed her a data slate filled with the security override codes she would need.

Armed and ready, she went down on one knee in front of her father.

'I swear I will kill Sudor and save our worlds, or die in the attempt,' she said.

She drew the edge of the sword across her left forearm, and let the drops of blood fall to the dusty ground.

A peculiar chorus of thumps rang around the gathered crowd; Bellori striking their unarmoured chests, witnessing her blood oath. Her father struck his own chest. His cheeks were dry, but his eyes were shining.

'I will make you proud,' she said, her voice steady.

'You already have,' he said. 'Go.'

Dray turned and walked out of the valley without looking back.

The cold winds of Zarix knifed her, but she welcomed them. She felt like them now, a force of nature, powerful and keen.

Four kilopaces of open, rocky terrain lay between her and Sudor's barracks. After only a few hundred paces, she felt the atmosphere around her change. Her thoughts seemed clearer and sharper in her own head, and that was when she knew she had passed out of Ayl's cloaking field. Nothing would hide her now but her own wits.

She made her way from rock to rock, staying in the

shadows, alert to any patrols that might pass. It wasn't long before a column of Nara-Kariths, led by a towering Meta-Karith, came tramping over in her direction, heading towards the volcanoes. Dray pressed herself into a narrow crevice in the ice-cold rocks until they had gone by.

Had the Bellori already been detected? No way to know. She must not think of them now. Focus the mind on one thing only.

She never stayed in the open for long, never broke cover without knowing exactly where she would move to next. She had done this countless times in holo-simulators during training, and in her dreams at night.

More troops of Nara-Karith and their Meta-Karith generals passed, but none of them saw her. She was a shadow, a fleeting movement in the corner of the eye. That was all.

When she reached the barracks, the main doors were grinding shut. Another column of Nara-Karith had just marched out. Dray, crouching behind a boulder, watched the last of them move out of sight.

Her back flat against the wall, out of the cameras' arcs of vision, she edged towards the door controls. This was the most difficult step. If the doors opened now to let more aliens out, there was nothing she could do but pray they didn't turn around.

There was a security camera above the panel, so that anyone using the intercom would be facing right into it. Keeping well out of its line of sight, Dray reached out from the side and felt the keypad with her fingers. Working by feel rather than sight, she tapped in the security override code.

A green light went on. The doors began to slide open.

Dray quickly ducked under the camera, round the reinforced gate pillar and through the doors. A quick press on the inside panel set them to closing again.

She was inside. She stalked up the winding ramp and stood outside the doors to the command dome, taking deep steady breaths. The final labyrinth lay within and had a monster at its heart. A monster whose head she was going to take.

Dray had killed many Nara-Karith, but never a fellow Bellori. On the threshold, she looked inside her own heart and asked herself if she truly had the will to do what had to be done. Because if she didn't, that weakness would betray her.

She punched her arm where she had made her blood oath. The sudden fresh pain from the cut burned her, focusing her senses to a single point. She was ready.

'I'm coming for you, Sudor,' she whispered. 'Not to capture. Not to interrogate. *To kill.*'

20

Perched high above the ground on a spur of rock, Keller watched the entrance to the valley through a Bellori visor. He couldn't have known it, but it was the very same perch Sudor had chosen to drill his forces.

Ayl had lifted the Aquanth shield after the trap was set. Now it was just a matter of time.

Come on, Keller thought. *Ayl dropped the cloak five minutes ago! Surely all those Bellori suits are registering on the base scanners by now! How long does it take you to muster for your main attack?*

Then he saw them, crablike, marching down into the valley. Iccus had been right about their numbers. There were thousands of the Nara-Karith, moving in a constant stream. Among them, striding like towering machines, were the Meta-Karith. Keller guessed at two dozen.

He scrambled down from the rocky ledge.

'They're coming, sir,' he reported to Commander Slarek.

The Bellori commanding officer gave orders to his squadron. 'Prepare to attack. Lieutenant Zhora, on my signal, activate the grid!'

'Yes, sir!' said the Bellori demolitions technician, readying her control pad. She was Keller's age, with hair in a shaved crest.

Keller licked his dry lips. His stomach felt tight.

More and more of the creatures were filing into the valley, marching in one long winding column like a river of swarming insects. Soon they would reach the empty armour.

'Hold your positions,' Slarek said.

The last of the creatures passed into the valley. Now the entirety of Sudor's force was here, ready to wipe out the Bellori soldiers with overwhelming numbers. *At least that's what we want Sudor to think.*

The Nara-Karith army began to attack the empty suits.

'They've taken the bait!' Keller yelled.

'Lieutenant Zhora! Fire the grid!' Slarek ordered.

The ground at the valley's mouth exploded. A row of concealed mines a pace apart sent constant, lacerating beams of energy into the sky, effectively closing the valley off.

'We've got them trapped,' Keller said with satisfaction. 'If they try to get out now, they'll be sliced to pieces.'

'Grenade launchers ready, sir,' said a voice behind him.

Keller gripped the hilt of the *scratha* sword General Iccus had given him. Just then, Commander Slarek ordered, 'Alpha Squadron! Open fire!'

Grenades rained down into the valley from both sides. The Nara-Karith teemed and scuttled here and there in confusion as explosive blasts shook their ranks apart. They still attacked the Bellori armour single-mindedly, picking it up and shaking it, gnawing at the arms and legs like wild beasts savaging prey.

Keller threw a frag grenade. The blast sent a Meta-Karith straight through the K-grid. Bright beams sliced it into chunks.

It's working, Keller thought. The aliens screeched as grenade after grenade ripped their bodies apart, turning the valley floor into a yellow-orange charnel house. *But for how long?*

The Nara-Karith were losing hundreds, then thousands of their number. Not a single Bellori had fallen. *Yet.*

'This is like shooting fish in a barrel,' Commander

Slarek said, sounding almost disappointed.

'I wouldn't be so sure,' Keller said, pointing. Most of the suits of armour had been torn to pieces now, and the Nara-Karith were turning towards the real threat.

We're going to have to go in. Now the real fighting starts.

'Charge!' Commander Slarek roared. The Bellori roared with him.

They surged down the side of the volcano, laying down pulse rifle fire as they went. The Nara-Karith screeched, struggling through the shredded bodies of their comrades to reach the Bellori.

The smaller Nara-Karith gnashed and ripped at the Bellori in the front lines. The lumbering Meta-Karith lashed out over their heads. Most often, the Bellori were quick enough to get out of the way. Some were not, and the thrusting claws killed them instantly.

They were whittling down the Nara-Karith numbers. Keller could see that. They were down to half their force now. But there were still so many, he wondered how they could ever destroy them all. From his left came a dying scream as Commander Slarek fell.

Keller was in charge now.

'Flank them!' ordered Keller. 'Units five and six, encircle that giant one. Open formation, keep moving.

Unit nine, suppressive fire!' The language of battlefield command came easily to him. *And my father told me I'd never learn anything from holo-games . . .*

Keller's commands attracted the attention of a looming Meta-Karith. Locking its attention on Keller, it came right for him, scrambling over the Nara-Karith in front of it.

'I know your game,' Keller growled, drawing his *scratha* sword. 'You think you've identified an enemy commander, don't you?'

The Meta-Karith's antennae bristled. A razor-sharp claw slashed at him, and he ducked out of the way.

'Guess what,' he said. 'You have.'

In a sudden bold move, he threw himself under the creature's body, between its bowed legs. Having worn Bellori armour, Keller knew that there were minute gaps between the armour plates. Aiming for one of these was his only hope. As the beast flailed around above him, Keller quickly stabbed upwards, driving the sword as deep as he could into the gap between the plates on its abdomen.

The Meta-Karith sprang away, screeching in pain. Keller scrambled to his feet. The alien lurched towards him and lashed out. With one stroke, Keller severed the claw that came lunging at his neck.

The creature seemed to sense it was losing the fight and could not understand why. It jabbed wildly at Keller, who threw himself to the side. The claw buried itself deep in the ground like an anchor.

Stuck fast, the wounded Meta-Karith struggled to pull its claw back out. Keller seized his chance and hacked the thing's head from its body in two quick blows.

It staggered and fell. Keller didn't have time to savour his victory. They were still coming, and the Bellori were dying in droves.

On the opposite side of the valley, Ayl was running down the slope beside General Iccus. The Bellori on either side of him were yelling a war cry as they opened up with their plasma rifles. The very air seemed smeared with blood. He wanted to scream.

Ayl could hear what the enemy was thinking, their orders screeching in his head as he desperately tried to override them. But there were too many of them, and the noise from the battle made it impossible to concentrate.

He didn't belong here. Nothing had prepared him for this. Aquanths weren't trained to fight! He'd thought a few experiences of pointing a k-gun at an alien and pulling the trigger would be enough, but he had no idea what to do with the bulky Bellori rifle he was carrying. He felt like a fish out of water, and he was scared.

But even through his own fear, he could sense what the Bellori were feeling. Without the protection of the armour they trusted, they were scared too. They could see their kinsmen dying in front of them.

I'm feeling the same thing as the Bellori, he thought in wonderment. *Who would have ever thought we'd have anything in common?*

He glanced down at the rifle again, trying to work out how to fire it. There must be some sort of safety catch still on. Maybe if he moved that toggle? Or he could just ask someone, so long as they weren't fighting for their life.

A green claw clamped round his chest. Ayl looked up in horror, straight into the grotesque face of a Meta-Karith.

It lifted him off the ground. Another claw came up and clamped itself around his ankle.

Ayl suddenly knew what was going to happen next – like the suits of Bellori armour, he would be torn limb from limb. He'd promised the Aquanths he would be their shield. Now they would all feel his death as the thing tore him apart.

But before the Meta-Karith could strike a lethal blow, General Iccus shoved his way forward. 'Move!' He drove a knife into a crack between two of the creature's armour plates and slammed his fist against the hilt for good measure, driving the blade in deep.

The Meta-Karith screeched, rearing up and dropping Ayl.

He could tell it was dying. General Iccus grabbed his arm and pulled him back away from it. The alien flailed, quivered all over and suddenly lashed out with a spear-like claw before falling heavily to the ground.

Ayl stared in horror. The claw had plunged right into General Iccus's chest.

'Medic!' he yelled. 'The general's hurt! Someone help!'

A great eagle-like bloodstain was already spreading across the general's tunic. Ayl tore the fabric open and felt despair as he saw the size of the wound. There had to be something he could do!

General Iccus's hand gripped his shoulder. The grip was like iron. The grey eyes fixed on him. A trickle of blood rolled down the side of his mouth.

'You're going to be fine!' Ayl said emptily, wishing a medic would come.

Iccus pulled him close and spoke into his ear. Blood rattled in the great man's lungs. Ayl knew with stone-cold certainty that these words would be his last.

'You don't need weapons to fight,' Iccus whispered. He sank to the earth, and his grip on Ayl's shoulder relaxed.

Ayl looked down at the body of the fallen Bellori leader, the father of his friend, and felt overwhelmed with confusion and despair. He could make no sense of those words.

Everyone here was fighting with weapons. Everyone except him, of course. He didn't even understand his weapon.

Maybe that was what Iccus meant. Maybe, instead of trying to fight like the Bellori, he should fight in his own way. But how?

He was a telepath. A *powerful* telepath, at that. And the Nara-Karith received their orders telepathically. He'd overridden their orders before, back on Cantor. He had to do it again now.

But there are thousands of Nara-Karith here! How can I control them? I'm only one person!

The answer came to him in a cold flash. *Sudor is only one person, too. And he's not even a natural telepath.*

Hoping the Bellori wouldn't think he was running

away, he headed back up the slope to get away from the noise. He reached the lip of the crater and huddled down on the other side, breathing hard.

He opened his mind.

The aliens' minds were thrumming with telepathic commands, echoing from one to another. *ADVANCE. ENCIRCLE. DESTROY.* It was like computer chatter run amok.

Ayl beamed his own thoughts into their minds, drawing on all the strength he had left: *SURRENDER. STAND STILL. STOP FIGHTING.*

Immediately he knew it was working. Some of the aliens were jerking randomly like puppets, their brains unable to process two sets of orders at once. He heard the Bellori yelling to one another, pressing the advantage.

Encouraged, he sent a fresh wave of commanding thoughts, sending more Meta-Karith minds into spasm. Then, without warning, a powerful force swept through the hive-mind of the Nara-Karith, reinforcing their original orders, rallying their scattered numbers.

Sudor.

Ayl recognized that cold, implacable will, and he knew it had recognized him. Their two minds locked in a battle of pure mental power.

Ayl struggled to keep the Nara-Karith confused, but he was flagging. He had very little strength left, he knew, and Sudor was just too strong. Still he fought, dragging up the last vestiges of willpower that kept his heart beating and his muscles working.

Turning back the bullets had almost killed him. Now he pushed himself past that point, harder than ever before. His heartbeat was slowing down, his limbs growing cold. He could taste his own blood now. From far away, he heard the sound of the battle. Death was coming, but like the Bellori, he would go down fighting.

Thank you, my people, he thought, reaching out to the Aquanths one last time, *and goodbye*. Then he gathered all of his remaining strength for a final assault on Sudor's mind.

He could feel Sudor's willpower battering him down. He could almost hear the man's laughter. Then, in one radiant instant, it was suddenly as if a waterfall of light was thundering down on him, filling every cell in his body to bursting point with pure energy.

Dumbfounded at his new power, he sent the Nara-Karith the mental signal of *peace*.

Their minds were instantly docile, frozen in abject submission. Sudor's thoughts went flittering away like a scrap of shadow, riding a shockwave of fury and disbelief.

Strength in unity, Ayl, his mother's voice said within his mind. *As I always told you. We stand together.*

Of course. It was *their* power he was channelling. All of Aquanthis had united to support him.

The sounds of combat from the valley were dying away.

Ayl walked down the hillside, hand outstretched. The focused power of Aquanthis radiated from him like an unseen supernova, rippling tranquility into the minds of the savage aliens below, commanding there to be peace.

Down in the valley, without any fuss, the Nara-Karith – and even the Meta-Karith – began to surrender, one by one.

Dray was inside the dome now. She knew the control room was very close. The corridors she moved through were empty of guards. Sudor must have mobilized all of them for his final crushing blow against the Bellori.

She found the last Meta-Karith outside the control room itself, standing guard. Typical Sudor. He couldn't bear to leave himself entirely defenceless.

Her silenced k-gun fired twice. The shots were deadly accurate.

Dray stepped over the smoking corpses to the control panel. She could hear Sudor shouting from inside the room and wondered if there were more troops inside. She used the master code to open the door, and slipped into the room.

Sudor was facing his bank of monitor screens, looking at his army standing inert.

'Obey my orders, you idiots!' he roared. 'I command you, fight!'

Dray could see over his shoulder that the Bellori were executing the neutralized aliens with single well-placed shots. She felt a thrill of wild excitement. The body of Sudor's army was finished – now she had to sever the head, as she had sworn to.

Sudor cursed and bent to open a storage cupboard set into the moulding beneath the row of monitors.

Dray recognized the boxes he was grabbing. They were emergency Bellori rations, to be distributed if the barracks was under siege and cut off from supplies.

'I don't think so,' she muttered to herself.

She could kill him now, just by shooting him in the back with armour-piercing bullets. He didn't know she was there. But that would make her no better than him.

Instead, she moved to block the door and kept her k-gun trained on him. There were no other routes out of the control room.

'Planning a trip, Sudor? You'll need to get past me first.'

Sudor spun around.

Slowly he raised his hands. Nutrient bars fell to the floor.

'Well played,' he said smoothly. 'I can see you're better trained than I imagined.'

Dray kept her pistol levelled at his head. 'I told you I was looking forward to putting a bullet through your face. It's time.'

'Guns, Dray?' Sudor glanced at her sword, and down at his own. 'Too afraid of a rematch?'

'This isn't a game. I'm here to kill you.'

'Yes. Yes, I see. You could certainly shoot me,' Sudor said. 'Like a good little girl, doing just what daddy told you to. Or you could grow up, stop trying to please the old man, and work with someone who already knows your worth.'

'What?'

'Join me, as my second-in-command.'

Dray laughed coldly. 'That's not funny.'

'It is a serious offer,' Sudor said. 'You're good, but

you could be so much more. I'll train you personally, give you opportunities that Iccus never will. What would you *choose* to be, Dray? An old man's bargaining chip, or co-ruler of an empire, feared by millions?'

Dray frowned.

'Don't be a fool!' Sudor encouraged her. 'You're a warrior, not a political pawn! Think of all the times the Cantorians and Aquanths have done something so utterly stupid that you've just wanted to slap them down. Why tolerate them a minute longer? Work by my side, and we can *rule* them! We can—'

Dray had heard enough. It was time to stop the violence raging outside, to put an end to Sudor for once and for all.

Sudor moved to grasp her gun, and in an instant Dray shot him three times.

He went flying back into the bank of monitors. Glass shattered and electric sparks flew. He lay there, unmoving.

Cautiously, Dray moved closer. She was using armour-piercing bullets, so Sudor's faceplate shouldn't have been able to protect him. Even so, she wanted to make sure he was dead.

His fist slammed the gun out of her hand. It went spinning away across the floor.

As Dray reeled, Sudor pulled out his sword with one hand. With the other, he reached up to his ruined helmet and wrenched it off his head.

His face was a horrific mess. One of his eyes was gone, a socket full of blood. The other eye stared down at her, full of vicious hate.

'Annoying, isn't it?' he hissed. 'When you try to assassinate somebody and they insist on surviving?'

Dray drew her own sword. 'Not for much longer.'

They began to circle one another, blades almost touching. So, Dray thought, it was to be swords after all.

Dray lunged, Sudor parried, and the fight was on.

She was keenly aware that she had no armour. Sudor's heavy blade could slice an arm or a leg off neatly. But she was faster than he was, and she darted in and out of his weapon's reach, striking at the cracks between his armour plates, trying to stay on his blind side.

Sudor fought without grace. There was only strength in his blows, and remorseless persistence. He tried to trap Dray against the wall, force her into a corner, battering at her with blows so hard she could not parry but only dodge.

Dray was soon panting hard. Sudor was like a robot,

unstoppable, unflagging. Her only hope was to stab him in the throat. But every blow she aimed to that area, he parried easily. She just had to get him to drop his guard.

She narrowly avoided a blow then made an expert feint, hoping to trick him into thinking she was striking his leg to hobble him. Sudor's blade followed where she had meant it to, leaving his upper body unprotected.

He couldn't parry now. Putting all her strength behind a single lunge, she thrust at his throat. But to her horror, Sudor smacked her blade aside with his armoured left forearm, leaving her overreached. She was badly off balance now and he knew it.

He slammed his sword down on her blade like a hammer, knocking it clean out of her grip and breaking the blade in two.

Suddenly Dray was facing Sudor, and she was totally unarmed.

21

Ayl looked over the smoke-wreathed battlefield. Never in his life had he dreamed he'd be witness to so much death and destruction. The remains of thousands of aliens lay broken and scattered over the torn-up ground, with the bloodied bodies of Bellori warriors sprawled among them.

The surviving Bellori were executing the last of the aliens. They were quick and methodical about it.

Ayl was aware he was looking at the carnage without feeling sick or guilty. It was ugly, and he knew he would never feel at home on a battlefield the way the Bellori did, but he knew he had done the right thing.

He had fought for a good cause, and he was proud. It was a strange, new feeling and he welcomed it.

A familiar figure was crossing the battlefield to reach him, striding through the thinning smoke. Ayl grinned as he saw who it was.

'Keller! You made it too!'

'Thanks to you, Blue. Don't tell me you had nothing to do with this!'

Ayl blustered. 'Well, I did have help . . .'

Keller was holding out his hand.

Ayl gladly went to shake it. Just before their hands touched, he turned aside, his face twisted up in pain.

'Ayl!' Keller said, alarmed. 'Are you OK?'

'Someone's trying to send me a message!'

'Who?' Keller asked. 'Is it Sudor?'

'Dray!' Ayl gasped. 'It's Dray, and she needs us – right now. She's in danger!'

A group of the Bellori under Keller's command flew them to the barracks in a heavy assault craft much like the one they'd used before. They touched down, and Keller ordered the Bellori to form a semicircle around the door.

'I want you ready to blow Sudor away the moment I give the word,' Keller said.

'Yes, sir,' said the lieutenant. The Bellori knelt and took aim.

'Dray's trying to talk to me again,' Ayl said, clutching his forehead. 'I think . . . I'm not sure what's going on, but I think she's about to come out. With Sudor.'

266

The doors were opening. Keller took aim with his own rifle.

Pushing Dray in front of him, holding up a small control pad, Sudor emerged from the barracks. Keller saw his destroyed face and guessed immediately what had happened.

But what the hell had he done to Dray? She was wrapped around with multiple Bellori webbing belts.

Belts with grenades on them.

'See this?' Sudor called, holding the pad where they could see it. 'This is a remote detonator. If I release my grip, whether it is because I choose to or because I am dead, it will activate and Dray will die.'

'Hold your fire!' Keller warned his troops.

'Shoot him, Keller!' urged Dray. 'You have to!'

'Here is what happens next!' Sudor yelled, interrupting. 'I'm going to walk on to that ship you just arrived in, leaving Dray with you, and I'm going to take off. None of you will attempt to stop me. You don't have time to take those belts off her, so don't try.'

'And then?' Keller demanded.

'I escape, of course. This detonator will function at anything up to planetary range. That means I can still blow her up until I warp out of the system, so don't think of sending any ships up after me!'

'What's to stop you taking her with you as a hostage?' Keller demanded.

'Apart from the fact that I hate the little scab?' sneered Sudor. ' She could contact your pet Aquanth telepathically like she did just now, and you'd track me down!'

'Keller, shoot him!' Dray pleaded, wriggling in the net of grenade belts as if she was trying to set them off. 'Don't worry about me! I'm not important . . .'

'Yes, you are,' Keller said, his voice trembling.

'You can't let him live. He's too dangerous to the Trinity System!'

'But you'll die!'

'I said I'd kill him even if it took my own life! I'll make that sacrifice! Just take him down!'

Keller raised his rifle. He could barely see because of the tears streaming down his face.

Dray closed her eyes. Sudor glared at him in disbelief. 'You wouldn't . . .'

'I would,' said Keller. 'Dray, I'm so sorry.'

His finger tightened on the trigger. One shot through Sudor's helmetless head, and it would all be over.

At least it would be quick.

'Don't do it, Keller,' said Ayl firmly.

'But she's right, Blue!' Keller said, helplessly. 'He's

too dangerous!'

'But Dray is too important to sacrifice,' Ayl said with a meaningful look. 'She doesn't know how important she is.'

'Just do it,' whispered Dray. 'Now. Keep the Trinity System safe.'

But Keller lowered his rifle.

There was no way he could kill his friend.

Dray stood as close to her friends as she dared, fighting to control her emotions. Sudor had smirked at her as the ramp went up on the Bellori fighter craft, a wad of freshly applied field bandage over his destroyed eye.

Now the craft was lifting off. She tensed, wondering if Sudor would take this opportunity to kill her after all. But in her heart she knew he would not. The whole Bellori army was watching now, and they could easily intercept Sudor before he could jump out of the system.

The moment his ship jumped, Sudor would no longer be able to detonate the grenades, and the Bellori ships would no longer be able to reach him. Even in the depths of her hatred, she had to admit it was an ingenious plan.

Yes, strategy was everything. Keller had been right that time he'd refused to land the ship and let her go in guns blazing. Raw strength wasn't enough.

She watched the ship become smaller and smaller, finally vanishing. Then there was a bright flash as the ship entered warp.

Instantly, Keller and Ayl were there by her side, cutting the webbing belts from her body with Bellori knives.

When they were sure she was safe, they led her away to another ship. For some reason, hundreds of Bellori were gathered there. They all glanced at her as she passed. It made her feel ashamed to be alive.

'I failed,' she said hollowly. 'I swore a blood oath, and my prey is still out there.'

'You'll still kill him,' Keller reassured her. 'You just haven't done it today, that's all.'

She put an arm around his shoulders and around Ayl's. 'Thanks. Both of you. Thanks for coming to help.'

'No problem,' Ayl said, with a gentle smile.

'You should have killed him when you had the chance, though,' she said. 'I mean . . . I'm glad to still be alive. But it was the wrong thing to do.'

'No, it wasn't,' said Keller. 'Ayl was right. You *are* too important. The Bellori need you more than ever now.'

Dray frowned. 'What do you mean?'

Keller put his hand on her shoulder. 'They need a new leader.'

Dray was puzzled. 'A new leader? But my father is the leader of . . .'

Her voice trailed off. She realized she had heard no reports of the battle. She had no idea of the casualties.

There could only be one explanation for what Keller was telling her, one reason why his face now looked so grave. Tears came, unbidden, to her eyes.

Keller and Ayl raised their fists to her in the Bellori salute.

Beyond, the first of hundreds of Bellori warriors did the same. Like a spreading wave, fists were raised throughout the Bellori army, saluting the new leader.

General Dray, ruler of the Bellori, wiped a single tear away where nobody but Ayl and Keller would see her do it. Then, her face stern and steady, she stood to face her people.

22

Dray looked down from the royal balcony at the crowded streets of Cantor. Beside her, Ayl was doing the same, though she doubted he was trying to spot potential assassins.

They were both in positions of honour, with a good view of the trade king's throne, which was currently occupied by Keller.

The Crown of Cantor was firmly in place on his head. He was busy reading some notes he'd made, getting ready to address the crowds.

'This is much nicer than last time,' Ayl whispered. 'That throne room was so stuffy!'

'I know Keller wants to make changes,' Dray replied. 'But don't you think he's gone over the top? Making the coronation into a street party, and inviting everyone on the entire planet?'

'They seem to be in a good mood, at least!' said Ayl, nodding at the upturned faces below.

'That's because Keller had the sense to lay on a feast for every district,' Dray said shrewdly. 'Don't expect that good mood to last once the food and drink runs out. He's got their attention, but he's going to have to offer them a lot more than free parties if he wants to make things right.'

Keller stood up and went to the edge of the balcony. There were no cheers. Vid cameras were pointed at his face. An expectant hush fell over the crowd.

'People of Cantor,' he said, his amplified voice echoing across the city. 'This is Trade King Keller. A great man once showed me that the right thing to do is not always the safe thing to do. I'd like to tell you about some changes that I believe will make our planet great once again.

'For too long, the rich have lived off the poor, forcing them to work in dangerous conditions. People have been traded like livestock, and beaten viciously. We have done shameful things.

'I have two things to say. Firstly, I am sorry. I didn't know.' He paused. 'Secondly, this ends. It ends now.'

Murmurs of amazement were breaking out among the crowd.

'Corporal punishment is to be outlawed,' Keller said, and the eruption of cheers from the streets nearly drowned out what he said next. 'Failing to provide decent working conditions will become a criminal offence.'

He had to pause for a moment and wait for the cheering to die down.

'To ensure that every citizen of Cantor can afford food and shelter I will be introducing a benefit system. How will this be paid for? The answer is simple: There will be a new tax on all trading.'

'He can't do that!' a merchant somewhere behind Keller whispered.

'Yes, he can,' said Tyrus stonily. Dray grinned.

'This is a plentiful world!' Keller declared, thumping the podium. 'We have more than enough resources to go around. The work of reform begins today. From now on, all Cantorians will share in our planet's natural bounty!'

Dray had to activate her helmet's noise filter.

The first session of the Trade Council took place after the speech. Trade King Keller took his place at the head of the table, wearing the Crown of Cantor. On his finger, his father's ring glinted in the light of a new morning.

'Ladies and gentlemen of the Trade Council, I call

this meeting to order,' he said.

Immediately voices called for his attention:

'Your Majesty, I need royal assent to open trade negotiations with the Vatrani—'

'My company urgently needs your signature on these exemption documents—'

Keller held up his hand for silence.

'The next person to speak out of turn will be removed from these chambers,' he said calmly.

The voices died down as they realized he was serious. The council members looked at him, unsure what to expect. This was not what they were used to.

'The first order of business,' he announced, 'is the abolition of slavery. Kindly turn to section four in your schedule, where you can read the new emancipation laws . . .'

The Trade Council meeting went on for hours, which meant that Keller missed much of the coronation celebration. But much to his surprise, he found that making new laws could be as exciting as eating and drinking.

When he finally made it to the grand hall, the formal feasting tables had been cleared away and the musicians were tuning up. Keller scanned the crowd, his heart giving a little leap when he finally spotted a figure in

Bellori armour standing off to the side. All day long he had been hoping for a chance to talk to Dray without someone else listening in.

He passed her a goblet of samthorn wine, and this time she took it. They clinked the goblets together.

'Congratulations,' she said.

'To the future?' Keller suggested.

'I'll drink to that,' she said, and did.

'Now, General.' Keller smiled. 'Might I have the honour of the first dance?'

'I'd love to accept,' she said. 'But I can't. I have to leave. There's a lot I need to attend to back on Bellus.'

'That's a shame, but I understand. Don't think you've escaped, though. There will be other dances.'

Dray tossed back the remainder of her wine. 'I can arrange for a new Bellori bodyguard for you, if you like.'

'Nah,' said Keller with a grin. 'If I can't have you, nobody else will do.'

Ayl saw his friends talking and smiling from across the room. As he moved to join them, he thought how nice it was to see Keller and Dray getting along for a change.

'Hope I'm not interrupting anything,' Ayl said.

'Blue!' Keller shook his hand. 'You're not leaving me too, are you?'

'Afraid so, Your Majesty,' Ayl said. 'Your irrigation tanks are great, but I'm dying for a proper swim.'

Keller chuckled. Dray smiled, but something was clearly bothering her.

'Dray?'

'All the violence you've seen – are your people ready for that?' she said.

Ayl shrugged. 'Honestly? Probably not. But why should I care? I'm not afraid to be different. I'm proud of what we did. The memories are still there, but they're not raw any more. More like scars.'

'Scars are badges of honour to my people,' Dray said warmly.

'Then that's how I'll see my memories,' Ayl replied. 'Anyway, I shouldn't be too hard on my own people. They did help. I need to thank them in person for that. And . . . there's one other thing I need to go back for.' He paused, not sure if he should say what he was thinking.

Keller raised an eyebrow. 'And that is?'

'I need to study the sacred texts on Aquanthis,' Ayl said. 'I've been thinking lately that the three of us . . . we're more than just friends. There's something special about us. I think we have a higher purpose, a destiny.'

'I'm not sure I have time for a destiny!' Keller laughed. 'I've got my hands full running a planet!'

'Me too,' Dray said, grimacing. 'Sorry, Blue. I'll be keeping my feet on the ground. Destinies and sacred texts are for Aquanths.'

'Are our three peoples really all that different?' Ayl teased, amusement sparkling in his eyes. Silently he sent them a mental message: *I used to think Aquanths were the only telepaths in the Trinity System, but you both seem to have the talent too. Makes you think, doesn't it?*

Dray and Keller traded glances.

Ayl just nodded and smiled knowingly to himself. 'I'll pray for you both. Rule wisely, my friends.'

He turned to go, then stopped for a last word. 'There's a saying on Aquanthis: "May the waters be warm and the waves be calm, until we meet again."'

And with a wink, he was gone.

Epilogue

The other Nara-Karith eggs had been tough, black, shrivelled things like ovoid meteorites. This one wasn't. It was smooth, soft-looking and translucent, much larger than the others. It looked *new*.

The other eggs were racked on shelves behind it, like the precious treasures they were. They were the only original Nara-Karith eggs left anywhere.

Unlike them, the huge soft egg had never been frozen in the vacuum of space, or been baked in the heat of a planet's core. It had never known any other environment than the liquid inside the cloning tank. The other eggs had all been squeezed out of the Nara-Karith queen's ovipositor. This one had been manufactured, the recipe drawn from the DNA of the other cells.

This egg was not empty. In the bright light of the laboratory, you could see through the shell to the maggot-like larva that lay coiled inside. It pulsed slowly, unmistakably alive.

A grin of triumph crawled across Sudor's mutilated face. He spoke into a recording module:

'*Batch eighteen is ready. The cloning process has succeeded at last. There is no longer any need for a queen. Full-scale egg production can now begin . . .*'

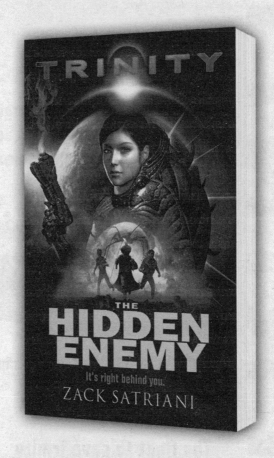

TRINITY

Dray, a Bellori warrior, will do anything to prove that a girl can fight.

Keller, a Cantorian master negotiator, will do anything to get his way.

Ayl, an Aquanth telepath, will do anything to keep the peace.

Thrown together on an asteroid far from home, these three must put aside their differences to save themselves, their parents and their planets.

Look out for the third book in the trilogy, *The Invasion.*

The fight to save Trinity has never been so dangerous ...

www.trinity-trilogy.co.uk
www.hodderchildrens.co.uk